"You're overwhelming, you're gorgeous, you're sexy."

Teal reached out and grasped Julie's wrist. "Don't play games with me—I don't like it."

"Some men might see the fact that I desire them as a compliment."

"I'm not 'some men.' And I'm damned if I'm going to spend half my time apologizing for that fact! You and I are *not* going to bed together, believe me."

Although born in England, *SANDRA FIELD* has lived most of her life in Canada; she says the silence and emptiness of the North speak to her particularly. While she enjoys traveling, and passing on her sense of a new place, she often chooses to write about the city, which is now her home. Sandra says, "I write out of my experience. I have learned that love, with its joys and its pains, is all-important. I hope this knowledge enriches my writing, and touches a chord in you, the reader."

Books by Sandra Field

HARLEQUIN PRESENTS
1506—SAFETY IN NUMBERS
1557—TAKEN BY STORM
1598—ONE-NIGHT STAND
1646—TRAVELLING LIGHT
1709—WILDFIRE
1739—THE SUN AT MIDNIGHT

SANDRA FIELD

THE DATING GAME

Harlequin Books

TORONTO • NEW YORK • LONDON
AMSTERDAM • PARIS • SYDNEY • HAMBURG
STOCKHOLM • ATHENS • TOKYO • MILAN
MADRID • WARSAW • BUDAPEST • AUCKLAND

ISBN 0-373-11762-0

THE DATING GAME

First North American Publication 1995.

Copyright © 1994 by Sandra Field.

This edition published by arrangement with Harlequin Enterprises B.V.

® and TM are trademarks of the publisher. Trademarks indicated with ® are registered in the United States Patent and Trademark Office, the Canadian Trade Marks Office and in other countries.

Printed in U.S.A.

CHAPTER ONE

HE WAS in a foul mood.

Teal Carruthers rolled down his car window. Several vehicles ahead of him, at the traffic lights, a delivery truck and a taxi had collided at the intersection; a tow truck and a police car were adding to the confusion without, as far as he could see, in any way ameliorating it. Behind him the cars were lined up as far as he could see. He looked at his watch. Five to five. He was going to be late home.

Today was Monday. On Mondays Mrs Inkpen came to clean the house and stayed with his son Scott until he, Teal, got home at five. Scott liked Mrs Inkpen, whose language was colorful and whose cooking bore no relation to the rules of good nutrition. Teal had gotten in the habit of taking Scott out for supper on Mondays, in theory to save Mrs Inkpen the trouble of preparing a meal, in actuality to protect himself from hot dogs adorned with anything from cream cheese to crunchy peanut butter. Even Scott, as he recalled, had not been too crazy about the peanut butter.

Mrs Inkpen didn't like him to be late.

The driver of the tow truck was sweeping up the broken glass on the road and the policeman was taking a statement from the truck driver. Teal ran his fingers through his hair and rested his elbow on the window-ledge. It was the first really hot day of the summer, the kind of day that made Scott, aged eight, complain loudly about having to go to school. Heat was shimmering off

5

the tarred surface of the road and the smell of exhaust fumes was almost enough to make Teal close his window.

The policeman shoved his notebook in his back pocket and began directing the traffic. Teal eased the BMW in gear and inched forward. Bad enough that he was late. Worse that he had had an interminable day in court. Worst of all was the fact that he had enough work in his briefcase to keep him up past midnight.

The traffic light turned red. He should never have trusted Mike with the brief today; that had been a bad mistake. A really bad mistake. Particularly with old Mersey presiding. Mr Chief Justice Mersey had been trying to trip Teal up for the last three years, and today he had more than succeeded. And all because Teal had left Mike, his brilliant but erratic assistant, to cross-examine one of the prosecution's main witnesses.

Mike, Teal now suspected, had been suffering from a hangover. In consequence he had been erratic rather than brilliant, and had committed not one but two errors of procedure. Mersey had had a field day chewing him out and Teal had been left holding the bag. Which meant he now had to rebuild their case from scratch. The only good thing about the day was that court had recessed until Wednesday. Tonight once Scott was in bed he'd have to get a sitter and chase down his two main witnesses, and tomorrow he'd catch up with the rest of them. Both nights he'd be burning the midnight oil to come up with Wednesday's strategy.

Who was he kidding? The three a.m. oil was more like it.

But Willie McNeill was innocent. Teal would stake his life on it. And it was up to him to produce enough doubt in the minds of the jurors so that they couldn't possibly bring in a guilty verdict.

It wouldn't be easy. But he could do it.

The light turned green. The traffic began to move and the bus that was two cars ahead belched out a cloud of black smoke. The policeman was sweating under his helmet, while the cabbie and the truck driver were laughing uproariously at some private joke. Very funny, Teal thought morosely. It was now ten past five.

By the time he turned into his driveway it was twenty-five past and Mrs Inkpen was waiting for him on the back porch. She was clad in a full-length pink raincoat with a hat jammed on her brassy curls, her pose as militant as an Amazon. Before Teal had married Elizabeth, Mrs Inkpen had cleaned for Elizabeth's parents, and he sometimes thought she should have been included on the marriage license. Although she was now well over retiring age, his tactful suggestions that she might prefer to be home with her ageing husband were met with loud disclaimers; she was fanatically loyal.

Bracing himself, he climbed out of the car. Mrs Inkpen tapped her watch ostentatiously. 'This'll cost you overtime, Mr C,' she said. 'If I'd known you was goin' to be this late, I could've cooked you a nice supper.'

At least he had been spared that. 'There was an accident on the corner of Robie and Coburg.'

Her eyes brightened. 'Anyone hurt?'

He shook his head, almost hating to disappoint her. 'A lot of broken glass and a traffic tie-up, that's all.'

'Drugs,' she said, nodding her head sagely. 'That's what it is, all them drugs. I said to my Albert just the other day, what with crack and hash and pot you can't trust no one these days. Never know when someone's goin' to creep up behind you and bash you on the head.' She rolled her eyes theatrically. 'Course you know all about that, Mr C, you bein' a lawyer and all.'

Mrs Inkpen's vision of what he did all day was drawn from television, and bore little resemblance to reality.

He said hurriedly, before she could ask him about his day, 'Can I give you a drive home to apologize for being late?'

'No need for that, I got to keep the old bones movin',' she said, her good humor restored. 'Smell the lilac, Mr C; ain't it a treat?'

Elizabeth had planted the lilac the year Scott had been born. Its plumes of tiny blossoms were a deep purple, the scent as pungent as spice. She had planned to plant a white lilac for the daughter that was to have followed Scott...

Wincing away from all the old memories, for there had been no daughter and now Elizabeth was dead, Teal said evenly, 'Lovely, yes...we'll see you next week, then, Mrs Inkpen.'

She gave him a conspiratorial grin. 'That nice Mrs Thurston phoned, and so did Patsy Smythe. It must be great to be so popular, Mr C—you don't never have to worry about a date on a Saturday night, do you?' The yellow daisies on her hat bobbed up and down. 'It's because you're so handsome,' she pronounced. 'Like the men in the soaps, is what I tell Albert—the ones the girls are always falling for. If I was twenty years younger, my Albert might be in trouble.' Cackling with laughter, she set off down the driveway between the tangle of forsythias and rose bushes.

The bushes all needed pruning. Scowling, because when was he supposed to find the time to get out in the garden and besides, Mrs Inkpen couldn't be more wrong—it was a damned nuisance to be so popular— Teal grabbed his briefcase from the back seat and went into the house. 'Scott?' he called. 'I'm home.'

The kitchen, starkly decorated in white and grey, was abnormally tidy. Mrs Inkpen achieved this effect, so Teal had realized soon after Elizabeth died, by opening the nearest drawer or cupboard and shoving everything inside. Any normal man would have fired her months ago. But he was fond of her, and loyalty worked both ways.

The telephone sat on a built-in pine desk by the window; the green light on his answering machine was flashing twice. His scowl deepened. One of those flashes, he would be willing to bet, was Janine, wanting him to confirm their date this weekend. Janine was nothing if not persistent. He didn't want to know who the other one was. He sometimes felt as though every woman in Halifax under the age of fifty was after him, each one certain that all he needed was a wife, a mother for his son, or a lover. Or a combination of all three, he thought with a twist to his mouth.

They were all wrong. He was doing a fine job bringing up Scott on his own, so why would he need to remarry? As for the needs of his body, they were buried so deeply he sometimes thought he should apply to the nearest monastery.

The telephone rang, breaking into his thoughts. Warily he picked it up and said hello.

'Teal? This is Sheila McNab, do you remember me? We met at the board meeting last week. How are you?'

He did remember her. A well-packaged brunette whose laugh had grated on his nerves. They chatted a few minutes, then she said, 'I'm wondering if you'd be free on Saturday evening to go to a barbecue in Chester with me? A friend of mine is celebrating her birthday.'

'I'm afraid that's impossible, Sheila; I already have plans that night,' he said truthfully.

'Oh . . . well, perhaps another time.'

'Actually I'm very busy these days. My job's extremely demanding and I'm a single parent as well . . . but it was nice of you to think of me, and perhaps we'll meet again some time.'

He put down the phone, feeling trapped in his own kitchen. Maybe he should shave his head and put on thirty pounds. Would that make the women leave him alone?

He heard Scott's footsteps thump down the stairs, followed by a swish that meant his son had taken to the banisters. The boy landed with a thud on the hall floor and came rushing into the room, waving a sheet of paper in one hand. 'Guess what, Dad?' he cried. 'There's a home and school meeting on Thursday, and you'll get to meet Danny's mum because she's going, too.'

Teal's smile faded. The last thing he needed was one more woman to add to the list. Especially such a paragon as Danny's mother. 'I thought home and school was finished for the year,' he said temperately, rumpling his son's dark hair.

Scott ducked, sending out a quick punch at his father's midriff. Teal flicked one back, and a moment later the pair of them were rolling around the kitchen floor in a time-honored ritual. 'Is that your soccer shirt?' Teal grunted. 'It needs washing in the worst way.'

'It'll only get dirty again,' Scott said with unanswerable logic, bouncing up and down on his father's chest. 'The meeting's so you can see our art stuff and our scribblers before school gets out; you'll come, won't you, Dad? Maybe we could take Danny and his mum with us,' he added hopefully. 'She's real nice; you'd like her. She made chocolate-fudge cookies today, I brought a couple home for you; she said I could.'

Janine, who had marriage in mind, had sent Teal flowers last weekend, and Cindy Thurston, who wanted something more immediate and less permanent than marriage, had tried to present him with a bottle of the finest brandy. He didn't want Danny's mother's chocolate-fudge cookies. 'I'd rather we went on our own,' he said. 'And you must change your shirt before we go out for supper.'

Scott stuck out his jaw. 'She's beautiful—like a movie star.'

Teal blinked. What eight-year-old noticed that his best friend's mother was beautiful? Feeling his antipathy toward the unknown woman increase in leaps and bounds, he said, 'There are clean shirts in your drawer. Move it.'

'She's prettier than Janine,' Scott said stubbornly.

Janine was a ravishing redhead. Teal sighed. 'I'm sure we'll meet her at the school,' he said.

And I'll be polite if it kills me. But just because her son and mine are fast turning into best friends it doesn't mean she has to become part of my life. I've got problems enough as it is, he added silently.

'Her name's Julie.' Scott tugged on his father's silk tie. 'Can we go to Burger King to eat, Dad?'

'Sure,' said Teal. 'Providing you have milk and not pop.'

With a loud whoop Scott took off across the room. Teal followed at a more moderate pace, loosening the knot on his tie. A sweatshirt and jeans were going to feel good after the day he'd had. He'd better phone for a sitter and drink lots of coffee with his hamburger so he'd stay awake tonight.

He was going to ignore both his phone messages until tomorrow.

Julie Ferris turned her new CD player up another notch and raised the pitch of her own voice correspondingly. She was no match for John Denver or Placido Domingo, but that didn't bother her. At the top of her lungs she sang about the memories of love, deciding that if even one of the men currently pursuing her could sing like that she might be inclined to keep on dating him.

Not a chance. On the occasions when her dates came to pick her up at the house, she sometimes contrived to have this song playing, *fortissimo*. Most of them ignored it; a few said they liked it; the odd one complained of the noise. But none burst into ravishing song.

It was just as well, she thought. She really didn't want to get involved with anyone yet; it was too soon after the divorce. Anyway, if the men she'd met so far were anything to go by, the options weren't that great. She was better off single.

'...dreams come true...' she carolled, putting the finishing touches to the chicken casserole she was making for supper. The sun was streaming in the kitchen window and the birds were chirping in the back garden. The garden was so painfully and geometrically orderly that she was almost surprised any self-respecting bird would visit it. On Friday she was going to find a nursery and do her best to create some colour and confusion among the right-angled beds with their trimmed shrubs and military rows of late red tulips.

Technically, her landlady had not forbidden her to do so. She had merely made it clear that she expected the house and the garden to be maintained in apple-pie order. An odd phrase, apple-pie order, Julie mused. A phrase she intended to interpret liberally.

The phone rang. Wiping her hands on the dishcloth, she crossed the kitchen to answer it, chuckling as Einstein the cat swiped at the cord with one large paw. She and Danny had only lived here for six weeks and already she had acquired a stray cat, an unkempt gray male who for the first week had eaten voraciously and virtually ignored them. Now, however, he was intent on running the household. She had called him Einstein because, despite his mass, he could move with the speed of light. 'Hello?' she said.

'Julie? Wayne here.'

She had had a date with Wayne last Saturday night; he was an intern at the hospital where she worked. They had seen an entertaining film she had enjoyed, had had an entirely civilized conversation about it over drinks at a bar, and then Wayne had driven her home, parking his sports car in her driveway. Before she had realized his intention he had suddenly been all over her, as if she were a wrestler he was trying to subdue. His hands had touched her in places she considered strictly off-limits, and his mouth had attacked hers with a technical expertise she had found truly insulting. She had pulled free from a kiss whose intimacy he in no way had earned and had scrambled out of the car, her lipstick smeared and her clothes disheveled. She had not expected to hear from him again.

'Julie—you there? Want to take in a film Friday night?'

Julie had, unfortunately, she sometimes thought, been well brought up. 'No, thank you,' she said.

'That film we talked about last Saturday is playing in Dartmouth; you said you hadn't seen it.'

She could lie and say she had plans for Friday night. She said, 'Wayne, I don't like having to fight my dates off. I'd rather not go out with you again.'

There was an appreciable pause. Then he said, sounding aggrieved, 'Fight me off? What are you talking about?'

'*I* have some say in who kisses me, that's what I'm talking about.'

'Hey, don't be so uptight—it was no big deal.'

'You felt like a tidal wave,' she said shortly. Large and wet and overwhelming.

'Don't tell me you're one of those feminists who charges a guy with assault if he as much as looks at them.'

Refusing to pursue this undoubted red herring, she said, 'I can hear my son getting home from school; I've got to go, Wayne.'

'What about the movie?'

'No, thanks,' she said crisply, and replaced the receiver.

Wayne was not the first of her dates to exercise what she considered liberties with her person and what they plainly considered normal—even expected—behavior. Robert had always told her she was unsophisticated, she thought grimly. Maybe he was right.

There was a loud squeal of brakes and then twin rattles as two bikes were leaned against the fence. Julie smiled to herself. Danny was home, and by the sound of it Scott was with him. A nice boy, Scott Carruthers, she decided thoughtfully. How glad she was that Danny and he had become such fast friends; it had eased the move from the country to the city immeasurably.

'Hi, Mum,' Danny cried, almost tumbling in the door in his haste. 'Scott fell off his bike and he's bleeding; can you fix him up?'

As Scott limped into the kitchen, any lingering thoughts about the peculiarities of male dating behavior dropped from Julie's mind. She quickly washed her hands at the sink, assessing the ugly grazes on Scott's bare knees. 'Danny, would you get the first-aid kit from the bathroom cupboard?' she said. 'That must be hurting, Scott.'

'Kind of,' said Scott, sitting down heavily on the nearest chair and scowling at his knees.

No two boys could be more different than Danny and Scott. Even discounting a mother's natural love for her son, Julie knew Danny was an exceptionally handsome little boy, with his thick blond hair, so like her own, and his big blue eyes, the image of Robert's. He was shy, tending to be a loner, and she had worried a great deal about uprooting him from the country village that had been his home since he was born. Scott, on the other hand, was a wiry, dark-haired extrovert, passionately fond of soccer and baseball, who had drawn Danny very naturally into a whole circle of new friends and activities.

She knelt down beside Scott, using a sterile gauze pad to pick the dirt from his scraped knees. Although he was being very stoical, she could see the glint of tears in his eyes. She said matter-of-factly, 'How did you fall off?'

'He was teaching me how to do wheelies,' Danny announced. 'But the bike hit a bump.'

Wheelies involved driving the bicycle on the back wheel only. Julie said, 'Not on the street, I hope.'

'Nope,' Scott said. 'Ouch, that hurts...my Dad said he'd confiscate my bike if he ever caught me doing wheelies on the street. Confiscate means take away,' he added, bunching his fists against the pain. 'My dad's a lawyer, so he knows lots of big words.'

The lawyer she had consulted to safeguard her interests in the divorce had charged her a great deal of money to do very little; Julie made a non-committal sound and wished Scott had practised his wheelies on grass rather than gravel. 'We're nearly done,' she said. 'I'm sorry I'm hurting you.'

'Do nurses always hurt people?' Scott asked pugnaciously.

Julie looked up, startled. There was more behind that question than simple curiosity. But she had no idea what. She said cautiously, 'They try very hard not to hurt anyone. But sometimes they have to, I guess.'

His scowl was back in full force. 'You work in a hospital; Danny told me you do.'

'That's right.'

'My mum died in hospital.'

Julie sat back on her heels. Danny had talked a lot about Scott but very little about his parents, she now realized. While there had been mention of a housekeeper—a Mrs Inkpen—Julie had assumed that the mother worked as well as the father, necessitating someone to stay with Scott. 'I didn't know that, Scott,' she said softly. 'How long ago did it happen?'

Scott looked as though he was regretting his outburst. 'Two years ago,' he mumbled.

'I'm sorry she's dead; you must miss her.'

'Sometimes I do, yeah . . . but my dad always took me to the soccer games, so that's still okay.'

The scrape on Scott's other knee was not nearly as dirty. As gently as she could Julie cleaned it up, then applied antibiotic ointment and two new pads. 'Use this tape, Mum,' Danny suggested.

The roll of tape had Walt Disney characters printed on it in bright colors. Julie used lots of it and asked, 'How does that feel?'

As Scott stood up gingerly, Danny interposed, 'I bet a popsicle'd make him feel better.'

Julie laughed. 'I bet you're right. I still have a few chocolate-fudge cookies, too.'

'We could go over to your place and play in the tree house,' Danny added.

'The cookies could be emergency rations,' Scott said, brightening.

'As long as you're home by five-thirty, Danny,' Julie said, packing two brown paper bags with cookies and juice, then watching as the boys wobbled down the driveway on their bikes.

So Scott had no mother, and Danny no father; maybe that was another reason why the boys had become friends. Even if Scott's father was a lawyer, he was doing a good job with his son, she thought generously, and went inside to slice the carrots.

The first Saturday night she was free, she might just take herself to see that film Wayne had offered to take her to. Alone.

One thing was sure: she wouldn't go with Wayne.

Because Scott had a dentist appointment at four-thirty on Wednesday, Teal left work immediately after court recessed. He hadn't let Mike say a word all day, and he'd been able to cast more than a reasonable doubt on several of the prosecution's main points. Which, for a man who had had less than five hours' sleep, wasn't bad.

He glanced at his watch. He didn't have a whole lot of time; the most difficult thing about being a single parent was the inevitable conflict between his work and his son's needs.

He navigated the traffic with absent-minded skill, and, when he drew up next to the house, honked the horn. The last thing he'd told Scott this morning was to be ready and waiting.

Scott did not appear. Teal leaned on the horn. He and Danny might be in the tree house, in which case they would have to scan the neighborhood, lower the rope ladder that kept enemies at bay, and then slither to the ground, clutching to their chests forked twigs that doubled as guns and slingshots.

But there were no bicycles leaning against the back porch. Impatiently Teal got out of the car, a tall, commanding figure in a pin-striped suit, and scanned the garden himself. 'Scott?' he called. 'Hurry up, we're going to be late.'

When neither boy appeared, he took the back steps two at a time and let himself in the door, which was firmly locked. There was a note propped on the kitchen table. 'School got out erly, a pipe berst,' it said. 'Gone to Danny's.'

His son might be a hotshot soccer player. But he was a lousy speller, Teal thought, and rummaged for the scrap of paper bearing Danny's phone number. He finally located it at the very bottom of the pile and dialed it quickly. A busy signal burred in his ear. Grimacing, he glanced at his watch and dialed it again. Still busy.

It was probably Danny's mother talking. In which case the phone could be tied up for hours, he thought with total unfairness. He'd better go over there right now. And he'd better hurry.

Danny lived six houses down the street in a stucco bungalow with a painfully tidy garden, which Teal disliked on sight. He parked on the street and marched up the narrow concrete path to the front door. The brass knocker was tarnished; Danny's mother wasn't quite the perfectionist that the garden would suggest. He pressed the doorbell and waited.

No one came. Through the open living-room window he could hear music, very loud music that was undoubtedly drowning out the sound of the bell. Feeling his temper rise, he pressed it again.

This time when no one came he pulled the screen door open and was about to pound on the door when the breeze wafted it open. Didn't she know this was the city, and that she should keep her doors locked? Stupid woman, he fumed. He went inside, wincing at the sheer volume of sound coming from the stereo equipment. Diana Ross, unless he was mistaken, singing something sultry and bluesy accompanied by a muted trumpet. It was not music calculated to improve his mood; he didn't want to hear a sensual, husky voice or the evocative slide of a trumpet over melancholy notes in a minor key. He had closed off that part of himself a long time ago.

Noises from the kitchen overrode the music. Teal strode down the hall and stopped in the doorway.

The four occupants of the kitchen all had their backs turned to him. Danny was leaning against the counter holding an imaginary trumpet, wailing tunelessly. Scott was perched on a stool licking cookie dough from his fingers. A scruffy gray cat was sitting on the counter next to him, washing its oversized paws much too close to the bowl of dough for Teal's liking. And, finally, a woman with a sheaf of streaked blonde hair held back by a ragged piece of purple ribbon was standing near the stove. She was singing along with Diana Ross, belting out the words with clear enjoyment.

Teal opened his mouth to say something. But before he could the buzzer on the stove went off, adding to the racket. The woman switched it off, swathed her hands in a pair of large mitts and bent to open the oven door.

She was wearing an old pair of denim shorts with a frayed hem, and a blue top that bared her arms and a wide strip of skin above her waist. The shorts must once have been jeans, which had been cut off. Cut off too high, Teal thought with a dry mouth, his eyes glued to the delectable, lightly tanned curves of her thighs, and the taut pull of the fabric as she leaned over to lift a cookie sheet out of the oven. He was suddenly angry beyond belief, irrationally, ridiculously angry, with no idea why.

'Perfect,' she said, and turned round to put the cookies on the rack on the counter.

She saw him instantly, gave a shriek of alarm and dropped the metal pan on the counter with a loud clatter. The cat leaped to the floor, taking a glass of juice with it. The glass, not surprisingly, smashed to pieces. The boys swerved in unison, gaping at him with open mouths. And the woman said furiously, 'Just who do you think you are, walking into my house without even so much as ringing the doorbell?'

Scott was right, Teal thought blankly. Danny's mother was beautiful. Quite incredibly beautiful, considering that she had a blob of flour on her nose, no make-up, and clothes that could have been bought at a rummage sale. He searched for something to say, he who was rarely at a loss for words, struggling to keep his gaze above the level of her cleavage.

'Hi, Dad,' Scott said. 'Boy, you sure scared the cat.'

'His name's Einstein,' Danny chimed in. 'Mum says that's 'cause he bends time and space.'

Teal took a deep breath and said with a calmness that would have impressed Mr Chief Justice Mersey, 'He certainly bent the glass—sorry about that. I'm Scott's father, Mrs Ferris . . . Teal Carruthers.'

'Julie Ferris,' Julie corrected automatically. Ever since Robert had walked out on her that last time, she had disliked the title Mrs. '*Did* you ring the doorbell?' she asked, more to give herself time to think than because she was interested in the answer.

'I did. But it couldn't compete with Diana Ross.' He added, wondering if her eyes were gray or blue, 'You should keep the door locked, you know.'

'I forget,' she said shortly. 'I'm used to living in the country.'

Why hadn't Danny warned her that Scott's father was so outrageously attractive? The most attractive man she'd ever met. Teal Carruthers wasn't as classically handsome as Robert, and looked as though he would be more at home in sports clothes than a pin-striped suit; but his eyes were the clear gray of a rain-washed lake, set under smudged lashes as dark and thick as his hair, and his body, carried with a kind of unconscious grace that made her hackles rise, was beautifully proportioned.

'Do you always let the cat sit on the counter?' he added. 'I thought nurses believed in hygiene.'

'Are you always so critical?' she snapped back, and with faint dismay realised that the two boys were, of course, listening to every word.

'If my son's to spend time in your house, I'd much prefer you to keep the doors locked,' he replied with an air of formal restraint that added to her irritation. What was the matter with her? She normally liked meeting new people, and certainly she had no desire to alienate the father of her son's best friend.

'That makes sense,' she said grudgingly, straightening the cookie sheet on the rack. Then she reached for some paper towel and knelt to pick up the shards of glass. Luckily they hadn't pierced the floor covering; she didn't think that would fall in the category of apple-pie order.

'I'll help,' Scott said.

As she stooped, Teal was presented with a view of delicate shoulderbones and the shadowed valley between full breasts. Her fingers were long and tapered, and the afternoon sunlight was tangled in her hair. He said flatly, 'We're late for your dentist appointment, Scott. I tried to phone you here, but the number was busy.'

'Darn,' said Julie. 'I bet Einstein knocked the phone off the hook again.'

Scott's face fell. 'I forgot about the dentist.'

'We'd better go,' Teal said, adding punctiliously, 'Thank you for looking after Scott this afternoon, Mrs Ferris. And for bandaging his knees yesterday—a very professional job.'

'The bill's in the mail,' she said flippantly, getting to her feet. Teal Carruthers didn't look the slightest bit grateful. And he had yet to crack a smile. 'I prefer to be called Julie,' she added, and gave him the dazzling smile she employed only rarely, and which tended to reduce strong men to a stuttering silence.

He didn't even blink an eyelash. 'Good afternoon,' he said, not calling her anything. He then nodded at Danny and left the room, Scott in tow. Julie trailed after him into the living-room, turning down the volume on the stereo as she watched a sleek black BMW pull away from the curb. It would be black, she thought. Black went with the man's rigidly held mouth, his immaculately tailored suit, his air of cold censure. Amazing that he had such an outgoing son as Scott. Truly amazing.

Her bare feet padding on the hardwood floor, she went to lock the front door.

CHAPTER TWO

THE home and school meeting was between six-thirty and eight on Thursday evening. Julie dressed with care in a plain blue linen tunic over a short matching skirt, her hair loose on her shoulders, and went promptly at six-thirty, partly because she had worked the last of her three overnight shifts the night before and needed to go to bed early, partly with a subconscious hope that she would thereby miss Teal Carruthers. Because of the connection between Danny and Scott it was inevitable that she would meet him sometimes. But there was no need to put herself in his path unnecessarily.

There was no sign of him when she got there. After Danny had shown her all his lively and inaccurate renditions of jet planes and African mammals, she chatted with his homeroom teacher—a pleasant young man she had met once before. The principal came over, a rather officious gentleman by the name of Bidwell, then the gym teacher and two school board representatives. It's happening again, Julie thought with a quiver of inner amusement. I seem to be gathering every man in the room around me.

The gym teacher, with all the subtlety of a ten-ton truck, had just revealed that he was newly divorced, when Julie glanced past his shoulder and saw Teal Carruthers. With another spurt of inner laughter she saw that if she was gathering the men he was like a magnet to the women. He was winning, though; he had six women to her five men.

23

'I wonder if I might give you a tour of our new computer-room, Mrs Ferris?' Mr Bidwell asked, bridling with old-fashioned chivalry.

'I'm sure Mrs Ferris would be more interested in the soccer facilities,' the gym teacher interrupted, giving his boss a baleful look.

'Actually,' Julie said, 'I'd like to meet Danny's music teacher—she's over there talking to Mr Carruthers. If you'll excuse me, please?'

Giving them all an impartial smile, she crossed the room to the cluster of women around Teal Carruthers. He was openly watching her approach, his expression unreadable. His lightweight trousers and stylish striped shirt were casual clothes in which he should have looked relaxed; he looked, she thought, about as relaxed as a tiger in a cage.

It was an odd image to use of a man so outwardly civilized. She gave him a cool smile, said, 'Good evening, Mr Carruthers,' and waited to see how he would respond.

With uncanny precision he echoed her own words. 'If you'll excuse me, please?' he said, flicking a glance around him. Then he took Julie by the elbow and walked her over to a display of books. 'I see you have the same problem as I do,' he said.

'You were one up on me,' she answered limpidly.

'But then you've only lived here just over a month.'

'You mean it's going to get worse?' Julie said with faint dismay.

Deliberately he looked her up and down, from the smooth, shining fall of her hair to her fine-boned feet in their pretty shoes. 'Very definitely, I'd say,' he drawled.

She was quite astute enough to realize he did not mean the words as a compliment. His fingers were still gripping her elbow, digging into her bare skin with unnecessary strength. 'I'm not going to run away,' Julie said, and saw with a primitive thrill of triumph that she had finally managed to disrupt his composure.

With a muttered word of apology Teal dropped his hand to his side, furious with himself for that small betrayal: he hadn't even realized he was still holding on to her. Standing as close to her as he was, it was no trouble to see why any red-blooded male under the age of ninety would be drawn to her, for besides being beautiful she exuded sensuality from every pore.

Her lips were soft and voluptuous, holding an unspoken promise that the imperious tilt of her cheekbones belied, a contrast that could be seen as both challenge and snare. Her body, curved and graceful, bore the same paradoxical blend of untouchability and beckoning. Although her height and slenderness made her as modern-looking as any model, her smile was both mysterious and ageless.

In the kitchen of her house he had wondered what color her eyes were. He now saw that they were neither gray nor blue, but shifting like smoke from one to the other. Chameleon eyes. Fickle eyes, he thought cynically.

'You don't like me very much, do you?' Julie said levelly.

He raised his brow. 'You believe in speaking your mind.'

'Life's short—it saves time.'

The women who pursued him always seemed to be smiling. Julie Ferris was not smiling. Suddenly exhilarated, Teal said, 'No—actually, I don't like you.'

Not wanting him to know that his opinion of her had the power to hurt, Julie chose her words with care. 'I was worried about Danny adjusting to the city and to a new school when we moved here, and I'm very happy that he and Scott are friends. It's really immaterial whether you and I like each other—but I wouldn't want our feelings to get in the way of the boys' friendship.'

'I'm quite sure we can keep meetings between us at a minimum, Mrs Ferris,' Teal said, and watched anger spark her eyes with blue.

'I certainly have no desire to do otherwise.'

'Then we understand each other,' he said. 'Ah, there's Scott's homeroom teacher; I must have a word with her about my son's appalling spelling. Good evening, Mrs Ferris.'

Julie watched him walk away from her. He was not a stupid man; he knew she didn't like being called Mrs Ferris. He had been needling her on purpose.

He really didn't like her.

Her thoughts marched on. In her kitchen she had labeled him as the most attractive man she had ever met. Attractive now seemed a flimsy word to describe him, and civilized a totally meretricious word. Sexy would have been more accurate, she thought shakily. Close up, the man projected raw magnetism simply by breathing; he was dynamite. As clearly as if he were still standing in front of her she could see the narrow, strongly boned features, the unfathomable gray eyes and cleanly carved lips. He had a cleft in his chin. His lashes were as black as soot. Not to mention his body...

Julie wriggled her shoulders under her tunic, trying to relax, and began searching the room for the music teacher. Dynamite has a tendency to blow up in your face, she chided herself. Dynamite is deadly. Besides, you were married to a man with charisma and you know darn well where that got you.

Learn from your mistakes, Julie Ferris. Which means, as Mr Teal Carruthers so succinctly phrased it, that you should keep meetings between you and him to a minimum.

An absolute minimum. Like none.

She caught the music teacher's eye and, smiling, walked across to meet her. Half an hour later, having assiduously avoided the gym teacher, she left the school with Danny and went home. She went to bed early, and woke up the next morning to the delightful knowledge that she had the next two days off. The sun was shining and the birds were singing...wonderful.

After Danny had gone to school, Julie took her coffee on to the porch and sat in the sun with her feet up. She felt very content. She had done the right thing by moving to the city, she knew that now. It had seemed an immensely difficult decision at the time, to leave the old country house where she had lived throughout her marriage; yet increasingly she had wanted more opportunities for Danny than the tiny local school could offer, and her own job at the county hospital had been in jeopardy because of cut-backs.

But there had been more to it than that. Inwardly she had longed to leave the house where she had been so unhappy, a house that had come to represent Robert's abandonment and betrayal; and she had craved more life, more people, more excitement than weekly bingo games and church socials.

She loved living in the city. On all counts except for the men she was meeting she had more than succeeded in her aims. Although she supposed there were those who would call her date with Wayne exciting.

She finished her coffee and went to two nurseries, loading her little car with flats of pansies and petunias and snapdragons. Home again, she changed into her oldest clothes and got the tools out of the little shed at the back of the garden. The spades and trowels were so clean she almost felt guilty about getting dirt on them. Almost, she thought happily, loosening the soil in one

of the geometric beds and randomly starting to dig holes
for the transplants. She disliked formal gardens. Too
much control.

An hour later the hose was sprawled on the grass in
untidy coils, the snapdragons were haphazardly planted
among the box-wood, and a fair bit of mud had transferred itself from the beds to Julie's person. Singing to
herself, she began scattering nasturtium seeds along the
edges of the bed.

A man's voice said over the fence, 'Good morning,
Mrs Ferris.'

The only person other than Teal Carruthers to call her
Mrs Ferris was her next-door neighbor, a retired brigadier
general called Basil Mellanby who lived alone and would
not, she was sure, ever make the slightest attempt to date
her. 'Good morning,' Julie called cheerily. 'Isn't it a
beautiful day?'

'Indeed it is.' He cleared his throat, rather dubiously
surveying the results of her labors. 'I have a measuring
stick if you should want to borrow it—just the thing to
keep the rows straight.'

His garden was a replica of her landlady's. 'I like
things messy,' Julie said apologetically. 'You don't think
Mrs LeMarchant will mind, do you?' Mrs LeMarchant
was her landlady.

'I'm sure she won't,' the general replied, with more
gallantry, Julie suspected, than truth. 'I had a letter from
her today; she's doing very well in Vermont with her
sister.'

And you miss her, thought Julie. 'How's her sister
getting along since her heart attack?'

The general chatted away for half an hour, then Julie
did her best to relieve the rigid straightness of the concrete path to the front door with masses of petunias,
watched by Einstein, who also liked digging haphaz-

ardly in the garden. Danny came home from school. She made supper and cleaned up the dishes, and when Scott joined them got the two boys to help her wind the hose and hang it on the shed wall. Then she went back in the house to get a drink of juice.

Einstein was crouched on the kitchen floor with a rat under his paws. The rat, she saw with a gasp of pure horror, was not dead.

She backed up slowly, fumbled for the screen door and edged through it. Her hands were shaking so badly she could hardly close the door.

Danny clattered up the steps. 'We're going to play cowboys,' he said and reached for the door.

'Don't go in there,' Julie faltered. 'Einstein's caught a rat.'

'A rat—wow!'

'It's not dead,' she added, wringing her hands. 'What will I *do*?'

If she called the general, he'd probably want to blow the rat's head off with a shotgun; the general had an immoderate fondness for guns. Or else, she thought numbly, remembering the network of tiny veins in his ruddy cheeks, he might have a heart attack like Mrs LeMarchant's sister. No, she couldn't ask the general.

'Aren't you going to get your holsters, Danny?' Scott cried, bouncing up the steps.

'There's a rat in the house,' Danny said with evident relish. 'Mum says it's not dead. Einstein caught it.'

'Jeepers . . . a real rat?'

'I can't go in there,' Julie muttered. 'I'm being a lousy role model but I'm terrified of rats.'

Scott let out a war-whoop. 'I'll get my dad,' he said; 'he'll fix it.'

'No, you mustn't——'

'Let's go!' Danny cried, and the two boys took off down the street. The rest of Julie's protest died on her lips because there was no one there to hear it. The general would have been better than Teal Carruthers, she thought grimly, and looked down at herself. Her sneakers had holes in them, her knees were coated with mud, and her T-shirt had 'Handel With Care' emblazoned across her chest under a portrait of the composer. As for her shorts, they should have been thrown out when she moved.

Inside the house Einstein meowed, a long, piercing howl that almost made her feel sorry for the rat. She shuddered. A half-dead rat on the white kitchen tiles could not by any stretch of the imagination be called apple-pie order.

A black car turned into her driveway, pulling up behind her small green Chevette. The boys erupted from it, and in a more leisurely fashion Teal Carruthers climbed out. He too was wearing shorts, designer shorts with brand-new deck shoes and a T-shirt so close-fitting that her stomach, already unsettled, did an uneasy swoop.

'What seems to be the problem?' he drawled.

'There's a rat in the kitchen,' she said, and through the open screen heard Einstein howl again.

'Sure it's not a mouse?'

In a flash of insight Julie realized what he was implying. The rat, in his view, was nothing but a trumped-up excuse for her to see him again. She was chasing him. Just like all those other women. In a voice tight with rage she said, 'I once accidentally locked myself in the basement with two live rats. Trust me, Mr Carruthers—this is no mouse.'

Teal picked up a pair of heavy gloves from the back seat and closed the car door. 'Two meetings in less than twenty-four hours hardly qualifies as minimal,' he said, climbing the back steps.

'I didn't ask you to come here!' Julie spat. 'Our two sons did that. As far as I'm concerned you can go straight home and stay there—I'll ask the brigadier general to come over; I'm sure he'd be delighted to blast his way through my house with a shotgun.'

'I'm here now; I might as well have a look,' Teal said. With a twinge of remorse he saw that she was genuinely pale, her hands shaking with the lightest of tremors. Mouse or rat, she'd had a fright.

She was wearing those goddamned shorts again.

'Can we come, Dad?' Scott begged.

'No, you stay out here...I won't be long.'

The two boys glued themselves to the screen door, peering through to see what was happening. Julie leaned back against the railing, taking a couple of deep breaths to calm herself, every nerve on edge. She jumped as Einstein emitted an uncouth shriek expressive of extreme displeasure. Two minutes later Teal pushed open the door, the rat dangling from one gloved hand. 'Have you got a shovel?' he said. 'I'll bury it for you.'

'I'll get it,' Danny said eagerly. 'Can we have a proper funeral?'

Teal took one look at Julie's face; she was backed up against the railing as far as she could go, cringing from the dead animal in his hand. 'I don't think so,' he said drily, and started down the steps.

Julie stayed where she was. Her knees were trembling and she had no desire to go inside and face Einstein's wrath. The last time she and Robert had been together, two rats had gotten in the basement of their house. Robert had laughed at her fears, neglected to set traps and announced that he was divorcing her for another woman. Two days after he had gone back to New York the latch at the top of the basement stairs—which she had twice asked him to mend—had trapped her in the basement. She had been there for four hours, along with the rats, until Danny had come home from school and released her. Even thinking about it made her feel sick.

When Teal came back, she was still standing there. He said tersely, 'Have you got any brandy?' She shook her head. 'Get in the car and we'll go over to my place— you could do with a good stiff drink.'

He was scarcely bothering to disguise the reluctance in his voice. 'Oh, no—no, thanks,' Julie said. 'I'll be fine now that I know the rat's not in the house any more.'

Teal gave an impatient sigh. If he had the slightest sense he'd leave right now. She was a grown woman, and definitely not his responsibility. He heard himself saying, 'Scott, go over to the house and bring back the brandy, will you? The dark green bottle with the black label. Put it in a paper bag and don't forget to lock the door again.'

'C'mon, Danny,' Scott yelled, throwing his leg over the seat of his bicycle. 'Let's pretend we're ambulance drivers.'

Wailing like banshees, the two boys disappeared from sight. 'I wish you'd go, too,' Julie said raggedly. 'You don't want to be here any more than I want you here.'

A lot of Teal's work dealt with the shady areas of half-truths and outright lies; he found Julie Ferris's honesty oddly refreshing. 'You look as though you're either going to faint or be sick,' he said. 'Or both. And I have to clean up your kitchen floor. Let's go inside.' Hoping it was not obvious how little he wanted to touch her, he took her by the arm. She was trembling very lightly and her skin was cold, and he felt a swift, unexpected surge of compassion. More gently he said, 'You need to sit down, Julie.'

Tears suddenly flooded her eyes, tears she was too proud to show him. She ducked her head, fighting them back, and made for the door. As she stumbled into the kitchen Einstein pushed between her legs in his haste to get outside. Teal grabbed her arm again. 'Careful—where in hell's teeth did you get that cat? It's got worse manners than an eight-year-old boy.'

'He got us—he was a stray,' she said with a watery grin directed at the vicinity of his chest, and sat down hard in the nearest chair. She averted her eyes while Teal wiped the floor with wet paper towel, by which time Scott had returned with a brown paper bag which he plunked on the counter. The brandy was exceedingly expensive. She gulped some down and began to feel better.

Teal topped up her glass and stood up to go. 'Call me if there's a replay,' he said wryly. 'It makes a change from legal briefs.'

The boys had gone outside. Julie stood up as well, and perhaps it was the brandy that loosened her tongue. 'Do you think I faked all this just to get you over here?' she asked. 'One more woman who's hot in pursuit?'

'You don't miss much, do you?'

'As a lawyer you deal with people under one kind of stress—as a nurse I deal with them under another. Either way, after a while you get so you can read people.'

Teal looked at her in silence. There was a little color back in her cheeks, and the tears that she had tried to hide from him were gone. He said slowly, 'It would be very egotistical of me to assume that you're pursuing me.'

'Indeed it would,' she said agreeably.

'You really are scared of rats.'

'Terrified.'

'Tell me why.'

'Oh, I don't think so,' she said. 'That's personal stuff.'

He felt a tiny, illogical flicker of anger. 'No, I don't think you're pursuing me,' he said. 'Despite the message on your T-shirt.'

Julie had forgotten about 'Handel with Care'. She flushed scarlet, the mere thought of Teal Carruthers touching her breasts filling her with confusion. 'It's the only dark-colored shirt I've got,' she babbled. 'I always seem to cover myself in mud when I garden.'

'I noticed that... I'm going to round Scott up; I've got a couple of hours' work to do tonight. Goodnight, Julie Ferris.'

She said awkwardly but with undoubted sincerity, 'Thank you very much for killing the rat.'

He suddenly smiled, a smile that brought his whole face to life so that it crackled with vitality. It was as though a different man stood in front of her, a much younger man, unguarded and free. A very sexual man, Julie thought uneasily, and took a step back.

'Just call me St George,' he said. 'Take care.'

Julie was still rooted to the floor when Danny came in a few minutes later. 'Einstein's sulking,' he said cheerfully. 'He growled at me when I tried to pat him.'

'I think we'll leave him outside for now,' she said with a reminiscent shiver. 'Shower night, Danny,' she added, and braced herself for the usual protests; Danny had an aversion to hot water and soap. Her best friend in the country had teenage sons who she claimed almost lived in the shower. Some days Julie could hardly wait.

On Saturday Julie turned down a date with the gym teacher, was extremely short with Wayne when he phoned, and went out for dinner with Morse MacLeod, one of the anaesthetists on staff. His wife had left him five months ago, a situation which could only fill Julie with sympathy. But Morse was so immersed in misery that he had no interest in hearing her own rather similar story; all he wanted was large doses of commiseration along with complete agreement that his wife's behavior had been unfair, inhuman and castrating. By the time he took her home Julie's store of sympathy was long gone. She was a dinner-date, not a therapist, she thought, closing the door behind Morse with a sigh of relief. But at least he hadn't jumped on her.

School ended. Danny and Scott added a new room to the tree house and Julie had to increase the hours of her sitter. The surgeon who had invited her to go sailing on his yacht at Mahone Bay, an expedition she had looked forward to, turned out to be married; his protestations about his open marriage and about her old-fashioned values did not impress her.

Her next date was with a male nurse from Oncology, a single parent like herself. His idea of a night out was to take her home to meet his three young children, involve her in preparing supper and getting them to bed, and, once they were asleep, regale her with pitiful stories of how badly they needed a mother. Then as Julie sat on the couch innocently drinking lukewarm coffee he suddenly threw himself on her to demonstrate how badly he needed a wife. Julie fled.

Driving home, her blouse pulled out of her waistband, her lipstick smeared, she made herself a promise. She was on night duty the following Saturday. But if that film she'd yet to see was still playing the week after that, she was going to see it all by herself. No more dates. No more men who saw her as a potential mother or an instant mistress. One bed partner, made to order, she thought vengefully. Just add water and stir. Did men honestly think women were flattered to be mauled on the very first date?

A traffic light turned red and she pulled to a halt. Not one of the men she had dated since she had moved to Halifax had been at all interested in her as a person, she realized with painful truth. They never got beyond her face and her body. Was the fault hers? Was she giving off the wrong signals? Picking the wrong men? Or was she, as the surgeon had implied, simply hopelessly old-fashioned?

The light turned green. She shifted gears, suddenly aching to be in her own house, Danny asleep upstairs, Einstein curled up on the chesterfield. She knew who she was there. Liked who she was. And if she was retreating from reality, so be it. She was thoroughly disenchanted with the dating game.

The Saturday after the rat episode Teal had dinner with Janine. He had met her at a cocktail party at the law school, and had then made the mistake of inviting her to the annual dinner and dance given by his firm of solicitors. It was considered bad form to go to the dinner without a partner, and he had rather liked her. Unfortunately she had fallen head over heels in love with him.

He was not the slightest bit in love with her, had never made a move to take her to bed, and once he had realized how she felt had actively discouraged her. All to no avail. Bad enough that she was phoning him at home with distressing frequency. She had now taken to bothering him at work. So tonight he was going to end it, once and for all. It was the kindest thing to do.

Great way to spend a Saturday night, he thought, knotting his tie in the mirror. But she was young. She'd get over it. She'd come to realize, as everyone did sooner or later, that love wasn't always what it cracked up to be.

Would he ever forget—or forgive himself—that on the very day Elizabeth had died they'd had an argument? Something to do with Scott, something silly and trivial. But the hasty words he'd thrown at her could never be retracted.

Irritably he shrugged into his summerweight jacket. He should pin a button to his lapel: 'Not Available'. 'Once Burned, Twice Shy'. Would that discourage all these women who seemed to think he was fair game?

This evening Janine had offered to cook dinner for him. He kept the conversation firmly on impersonal matters throughout the meal, told her as gently as he could that he didn't want to hear from her again, and patiently dealt with her tears and arguments. He was home by ten. Thoroughly out of sorts, he paid the sitter and poured himself a glass of brandy.

Swishing it around the glass, absently watching the seventh inning of a baseball game on television, he found himself remembering Julie Ferris. Her fear of rats had reduced her to tears. But she had hated crying in front of him, and would be, he was almost sure, totally averse to using tears as a weapon. Unlike Janine. But then, unlike Janine, Julie Ferris wasn't in love with him. She didn't even like him.

He hadn't been strictly truthful when he had said he didn't like her. He did like her honesty.

His hands clenched around the glass as he remembered other things: the sunlight glinting in the shining weight of her hair; the way she had trembled at the sight of the rat; her incredibly long legs and the fullness of her breasts under the mud-stained T-shirt that said 'Handel with Care'.

His body stirred to life. With an exclamation of disgust he changed the channel to a rerun of *Platoon* and immersed himself in its claustrophobic tale of war and death.

He was going to stay away from Julie Ferris.

And for two weeks he did just that. But he wasn't always as successful at keeping her out of his thoughts. At a barbecue in Mike's back yard a young woman called Carole attached herself to him, agreeing with everything he said, laughing sycophantically at all his jokes; Julie's level gaze and caustic tongue were never far from Teal's mind. Then Marylee and Bruce, two of his oldest and most cherished friends, invited him to spend the day at their summer cottage on the Northumberland Strait.

'Can I ask Danny?' Scott said immediately. 'We could go swimming and play tennis, hey, Dad?'

'No,' Teal said, the reply out of his mouth before he even had time to think about it.

'Why not?' Scott wailed.

Teal didn't know why. Because he didn't want to explain to Bruce and Marylee who Danny was? Because he didn't want to phone Julie and tell her about the outing? Because he didn't want to feel that he should ask her as well?

Knowing he was prevaricating and not liking himself very much for doing it, Teal said, 'We can't go everywhere with Danny, son. And his mother might not like us driving all that distance and being late home. Maybe another time.'

Scott stuck his lower lip out and ran up the stairs, slamming the door to his room. Teal raked his fingers through his hair. He should discipline Scott for his behavior. But somehow he didn't have the heart to do so.

Logically, Julie Ferris was exactly the woman he should be taking with him to the cottage. She wasn't interested in him. She wouldn't be phoning him all the time or trying to give him presents he didn't want. She wouldn't be doing her best to entice him into her bed.

Restlessly he prowled around the room, picking up the scattered pages of the newspaper and a dirty coffee-mug. So why wasn't he phoning her and suggesting that she and Danny accompany them? It would be a foursome. Quite safe.

Like a family, he thought, standing stock-still on the carpet. A husband and a wife and their two children.

No wonder he wasn't picking up the telephone—the picture he had conjured up hit much too close to home. But there was no way he could explain to Scott the real reason why Danny and Julie Ferris couldn't go with them.

The cottage on a sunny afternoon in July was an extremely pleasant place to be. Scott was playing in the swimming-pool with Sara and Jane, Bruce and Marylee's two daughters, while the adults lay on the deck overlooking the blue waters of the strait, drinking rum fizzes and gossiping lazily about some of their colleagues, one of whom was having a torrid affair with a female member of parliament. Marylee, a brunette with big green eyes, said casually, 'Are you involved with anyone, Teal?' As he shook his head she tilted her sunhat back the better to see his face. 'It's two years since Elizabeth died...isn't it time?'

Glad that his dark glasses were hiding his eyes, Teal said fliply, 'Nope.'

Reflectively she extracted a slice of orange from her glass and chewed on it. 'Even if you don't want to get involved, that's no reason to eschew female company.'

'I don't,' he said, stung. 'Next Friday I'm going to a medical convention dance with a surgeon who's definitely female.' He had wondered if Julie Ferris might also be going. But he wasn't going to share that with Marylee.

Wrinkling her tip-tilted nose, Marylee said, 'And I bet you five dollars that'll be your first and last date with the surgeon.'

'I'm not interested in another relationship,' Teal said tightly.

'You must have lots of offers.'

'Too many.'

'Well, you're a very sexy man,' she said seriously. Bruce, stretched out beside her, gave a snort of laughter. Ignoring him, she added, 'Plus you're a good father and a fine lawyer—you have integrity.'

Embarrassed, Teal said comically, 'I don't think the women are chasing me because of my integrity.'

'It's your body and your bank account—in that order,' Bruce put in.

'Stop joking, you two,' Marylee said severely. 'Grief is all very well, Teal, but Scott needs a mother. And it's not natural for you to live like a monk.'

Grief Teal could handle. It was the rest he couldn't. 'I'm not ready for any kind of commitment, Marylee,' he said, getting up from his chair and stretching the tension from his body. 'Who's going for a swim?'

'Men,' Marylee sniffed. 'I'll never understand them if I live to be a hundred.'

Bruce pulled her to her feet. 'You shouldn't bother your pretty little head over us, baby doll,' he leered. 'Barefoot and pregnant, that's your role in life.'

'Men have been divorced for less than that,' Marylee said darkly, then giggled as Bruce swept her off her feet with a passionate kiss.

Teal looked away, conscious of a peculiar ache in his belly. Although Bruce and Marylee had been through some struggles in their marriage, he would stake his life that the marriage was sound. Yet it hurt something deep within him to witness the love they shared.

Love . . . that most enigmatic and elusive of emotions.

No wonder he didn't want to get involved, he thought, and headed for the pool.

CHAPTER THREE

JULIE FERRIS was on Teal's mind again the following Friday when he and Dr Deirdre Reid entered the banquet hall in the hotel. He found himself searching the crowd for a crown of gleaming blonde hair, and didn't know whether he was disappointed or relieved when he couldn't find the tall, strikingly beautiful woman who was the mother of his son's best friend. His companion said something to him, then tugged at the sleeve of his tuxedo. 'Who are you looking for?'

'It's always interesting to see how many people I know at affairs like this,' he said vaguely. 'Do you have any idea where we're sitting?'

'At the head table—I told you I'm the president of the local association,' Deirdre said briskly, and began threading her way through the throng of people.

Grinning to himself, not at all surprised that they were at the head table, Teal followed. One reason he'd accepted Deirdre's invitation was because he didn't think there was any danger she'd fall in love with him; Deirdre Reid's emotions were very much under control. If indeed she had any. There were times when her acerbic sense of humor made him wonder. But she was good company, intelligent and well-informed politically.

He was introduced to a great many medical pundits on the way to the head table, where the meal was interjected with speeches, all fortunately brief, some very witty. But it was not until the dancing began in the next room that he saw the woman he had subconsciously been searching for all evening.

42

Julie Ferris. She was jiving with a tall, strikingly good-looking young man. She danced as if there were no tomorrow, every movement imbued with grace, joyous in a way that made his throat close. Her unselfconscious pleasure seemed to embody something he had lost—if indeed he had ever had it. He said, without having thought out the question at all, 'Who's the tall guy with the red hair?'

Deirdre followed his gaze. With a malicious smile she said, 'The youngest and most brilliant specialist on staff—neurosurgery—and the worst womanizer. Why do you ask?'

'I know the woman he's with.'

Deirdre said dismissively, 'He'll be bedding her before the night's out, I'm sure. She's rather pretty, isn't she? Shall we dance?'

So Julie Ferris liked sex. As much as the women who chased him. She just had a different man in mind; he, Teal, had not turned her on. Turning his back on her, he whirled Deirdre in a circle and began to dance.

The band was excellent and the wine had flowed freely during the meal. The crowd ebbed and flowed, the laughter ever louder, the colors of the women's dresses as bright as summer flowers, but not, Teal thought sardonically, as innocent. Smoothly he traversed the dance-floor, Deirdre following his every move with a clockwork precision. The waltz ended. Julie and her partner were standing not ten feet away from them, the neuro-surgeon's hand placed familiarly low on her hip. Teal said clearly, 'Hello, Julie.'

Her head swung round. 'Teal... I noticed you were here,' she said, and removed the doctor's hand.

'I'd like you to meet Dr Deirdre Reid,' Teal said. 'Julie Ferris, Deirdre... her son and mine are friends.'

'Dr Reid and I have already met,' Julie said coolly, her smile perfunctory.

'Ferris?' Deirdre repeated with equal coolness. 'Oh, of course, Men's Surgical. I didn't recognize you out of uniform; all nurses look alike to me.' She smiled up at Julie's partner. 'Hello, Nick, how are you? Teal Carruthers...Dr Nicholas Lytton.'

The young neurosurgeon had very pale blue eyes, and Teal disliked him on sight. As the band struck up a slow foxtrot, he said, 'Dance with me, Julie?'

The twin patches of scarlet in her cheeks matched her outfit—a silk dinner-suit with a flounced neckline and glittering buttons; her hair was upswept on her crown, elaborate gold earrings swaying from her lobes. 'Thank you,' she said, and moved into his arms.

While the color in her cheeks could have stemmed from Deirdre's rudeness, Teal thought that more probably it was in anticipation of ending the night in the neurosurgeon's bed. She felt very different from Deirdre in his embrace, her body lissome, utterly in tune with the languorous, sensual music. He led her through a complicated turn and said, 'You know you're dating the worst womanizer in the entire hospital?'

Her head jerked up. Her eyes, he saw, were sparked blue with temper. 'Who told you that?'

'Deirdre.'

'Is she speaking from personal experience?'

Teal gave a choked laugh. 'It's not like you to be bitchy.'

'You have no idea what I'm like.'

The question forced itself past his lips. 'Are you going to bed with him, Julie?'

'Really, Teal, what kind of a question is that?'

'A fairly straightforward one, I would have thought.'

'You're not in court—this is no place for a cross-examination,' she said, and her lips—very kissable lips—compressed in a way that made his hands tighten their hold. 'Don't grab me,' she added crossly.

'Why not? Because I'm not a brilliant neurosurgeon, just a lawyer, and they're a dime a dozen?'

'Boy, you're sure spoiling for a fight, aren't you? Not that I'm surprised. Three hours of Dr Reid would put a saint in a bad mood.'

'She's an intelligent and attractive woman.'

'So are you going to bed with her, Teal?' she parried nastily.

'No,' he announced. 'Why was she so rude to you?'

'On my last shift she yelled at me in front of several interns and two other doctors for a mistake I hadn't made. When I pointed out her error, she declined to apologize.' Julie sniffed. 'She treats patients like collections of removable organs and nurses like dirt.'

Somehow Teal had no trouble believing every word Julie had just said. 'Then we agree about something,' he remarked.

'What's that?' she asked suspiciously.

'Neither of us likes the other's choice of a date.'

'You have no reason to dislike Nick,' she flashed.

He remembered the hand sliding down her hip and said curtly, 'Danny deserves better of you than someone like Nick.'

'Danny's got nothing to do with it!'

'So you don't take your men home when you go to bed with them? How discreet of you,' he sneered, recognizing with a distant part of his brain that he was behaving reprehensibly.

'What have you got against me, Teal?' Julie demanded. 'You've disliked me from the minute we met.'

You're beautiful and full of life and you're driving me crazy...

For a horrible moment Teal thought he had spoken the words out loud. 'Just don't expose my son to your love life—that's an order,' he said coldly. 'He likes you and I wouldn't want him thinking promiscuity is acceptable adult behavior.'

'I promise that when I stand on a street corner soliciting it won't be your street,' she snapped. 'It's beyond me how you have such a nice son! Since—like most men—you're totally wrapped up in your job, I can only presume that your wife brought Scott up.'

She felt Teal's instant response through her fingers: a tightening of his shoulder muscles, a rigidity in his spine. 'Leave my wife out of this,' he grated. 'She's none of your business and never will be. And now I'd better hand you back to Nick, hadn't I? I wouldn't want the two of you to waste any time.'

As the saxophone whispered its last chords and the dancers clapped he led her toward the other couple. 'Yours, I believe,' he said to Nick, and smiled rather more warmly than he had intended at Deirdre. 'Why don't we take a break and get a drink?' he suggested, and without a backward look threaded his way off the dance-floor.

There were two other couples that Teal knew at the bar, and they got into a ribald discussion on senate reform. An hour later when he and Deirdre went back to the ballroom, there was no sign of Nick and Julie.

They've gone to his place, Teal thought viciously, and wondered why in God's name it mattered to him. Almost as though she'd read his mind Deirdre said, 'Why don't we go to my apartment for a nightcap, Teal? I've just about had enough of this.' So he wouldn't mistake her meaning, she traced his lower lip with her finger, her eyes a mingling of mockery and seduction.

He removed her hand. 'I'm not into casual sex, Deirdre.'

'It's the only kind worth having.'

'Not for me...sorry.'

'I could change your mind.'

He gave her a smile every bit as mocking as her own. 'Haven't you heard that no means no?'

'What a liberated man you are, Teal,' she responded, with no intent to flatter. 'Tell the truth—if I were Julie Ferris, no would mean yes. Because you'd rather be standing in Nick's shoes than your own right now. Not that I can imagine Nick's still wearing his shoes.'

Teal felt a surge of pure fury. Battling it down, he said, 'I'll take you home.' And I won't go out with you again, he thought. Thank you very much.

Fifteen minutes later, having left Deirdre in the lobby of her apartment building, he drove past Julie's bungalow. There was a light on in the living-room and her car was the only one parked in the driveway. So he was right. She wouldn't risk Danny waking up. She'd conduct her affairs elsewhere, with discretion.

He sent the sitter home in a cab, poured himself a brandy and scowled at the antics of the Harlem Globetrotters on the television. Maybe Deirdre was right. Casual sex was the only kind worth having.

It would beat sitting here trying not to think about Julie Ferris.

A week later Julie finally took herself over to Dartmouth to see the film she'd refused to go and see with Wayne. She'd been shopping with Danny earlier in the day, had arranged a sitter for eight-fifteen, and got to the mall with twenty minutes to spare. The theater was inside the mall. There was a line-up for tickets, because several movies were playing at the same time. She got behind two young men in neon-tinted T-shirts and fumbled for her money, rather pleased with herself that she had come on her own.

Someone jostled her arm. As she looked up, surprised, the boy in the fluorescent green shirt, who had close-set eyes of an indeterminate shade of gray, said, 'Hey, babe, where's your date?'

'I don't have one,' she said shortly, and closed her purse.

The second one, whose T-shirt logo should have been banned for obscenity, laughed coarsely. 'There's two of us; we'll look after you,' he said, and added something that in crudity far surpassed the message on his shirt.

Neither of them was a day over seventeen. But they were taller than she, seething with unfocussed energy and smelling strongly of beer; Julie smothered her temper and turned her head away.

'Sure,' said the first one, 'we'll sit with you, won't we, Hank? Keep you company. Who wants to be alone on a Saturday night?'

'I do,' said Julie.

'Which movie you going to?' Hank asked, and grabbed for her elbow, his knuckles brushing her breast.

He had done it on purpose. Utterly furious, because the last thing she wanted was to be ogled by two young men in the combined thrall of alcohol and hormones, Julie said, 'Let me alone—or I'll have you thrown out of the theater.'

Hank straightened. 'You and who else?' he sneered.

'How about me?' said a voice behind Julie.

She whirled, knowing exactly who she was going to see. Teal Carruthers was standing on the fringe of the queue dressed in a faded denim shirt and jeans. He wasn't looking at her; his gaze was trained on Hank, and something in his stance kept Hank silent. Teal's energy was both contained and focussed, Julie thought uncertainly, and he looked ten times more dangerous than Hank.

Teal said evenly, 'You can shut up and leave her alone. Or you can leave the line-up—which is it to be?'

'Man, we were only kidding,' Hank's companion said uneasily. 'We weren't——'

'It didn't look that way to me,' Teal interrupted. 'Make your minds up.'

Hank, like most bullies, had finely tuned antennae for those stronger than himself. 'We weren't really planning to sit with her; we were only having a little fun.'

'I'd suggest you keep your sense of humor to yourself from now on,' Teal said.

'We'll leave her alone,' Hank answered sulkily.

As the two boys turned their backs, the line inched forward, and Julie said with a noticeable lack of sincerity, 'Thank you. Now you'd better go back to your date.'

'Haven't got one.'

So he wasn't here with Deirdre Reid. 'Goodness,' Julie said sweetly, 'is your phone out of order?'

'Not that I'm aware of. Has Einstein knocked yours off the hook?'

'*I* was endeavouring to have a quiet Saturday night without being hassled by anyone. Which includes you.'

'Rescuing you is getting to be a habit,' Teal responded. 'You're a walking trouble zone.'

'Are you insinuating I'm responsible for what just happened?' Julie blazed.

Unwisely Teal spoke the exact truth. 'You're very beautiful when you're in a rage,' he said.

'Oh!' she exclaimed between gritted teeth. 'I can't *stand* men! In particular I can't stand you. Go away!'

Discovering that he was thoroughly enjoying himself, and that it was going to have to be an exceedingly good movie to beat the pre-movie entertainment, Teal said, 'I've lost my place in the line by now.'

'You think you're pretty clever, don't you?'

'I came here to be on my own, too,' he said mildly, and watched her assess that piece of information.

'Don't tell me you can't stand women—I won't believe you.'

'But I'm supposed to believe you when you say you can't stand men? I'd hate to find you guilty of sexism, Julie.'

'You're a fine one to talk about sexism—accusing me of promiscuity just because I was dancing with Nick!' Not until she actually spoke did Julie realize how much that remark had rankled.

Ahead of her Hank and his cohort were buying their tickets; they were going to the latest horror film. Julie bought her own ticket and with a strange sense of fatalism heard Teal ask for the same movie. As they walked past the usher and into the lobby, she said, glaring at him, 'I suggest we sit at opposite ends of the theater.'

Teal thrust his hands in his pockets. 'I have no real evidence that you're promiscuous. I shouldn't have said that—I'm sorry.'

It was, in Julie's opinion, a fairly minimal apology. 'So why did you?' she demanded.

'I've said I'm sorry, Julie.'

She bit her lip. 'All right,' she said grudgingly. 'Just don't do it again.'

'So do you really want us to sit at opposite ends of the theater?'

If she was smart she'd say yes. She looked straight into his guarded gray eyes and said, knowing this was important, 'You haven't answered my question—whether

I'm responsible for the behavior of those two louts. I don't like being called a trouble zone, Teal. *I'm* not the cause of the trouble. Look at me—you can't say I'm dressed as if I'm looking for trouble.'

Her jeans, while slim-fitting, were not tight; her white shirt was tailored, her hair pulled back with a plain velvet ribbon. Teal looked at the full curve of her lip and the push of her breasts against the white cotton and said, 'It wouldn't matter what you wore, Julie—you've got that indefinable something called sex appeal. You're loaded with it. Any man who doesn't have one foot in the coffin and the other on a banana peel is going to react.'

She frowned at him. 'So it *is* my fault.'

'Of course it's not—I'm explaining, not excusing. I've handled enough rape cases not to buy the line that says the woman asked for it and the man's not responsible for his actions. It stinks.'

'I see,' said Julie, looking at him through narrowed eyes. 'If you really believe what you just said, I'm delighted—the justice system needs more like you. But if not, then I've caught you out. Because—to use your own logic—Nick's being a womanizer doesn't automatically make me promiscuous.'

'I should never have said that, okay? And that's the last apology you're getting!'

The turbulence in his eyes was having a most peculiar effect on her. 'If I've got sex appeal,' she said recklessly, 'so have you. Tons of it. Truckloads of it. And don't pretend I'm the first woman to tell you so.'

Marylee had used the word sexy; but she'd meant the same thing. Teal said smoothly, 'Then maybe we should sit together for our mutual protection,' and watched the first hint of laughter glint in Julie's face. Like a tiny explosion in his brain he felt an idea spring to life.

'Only if you like popcorn,' she replied.

'You mean I have to admit to all my addictions in order to sit with you?'

This time she laughed outright. 'Two large buttered popcorn coming up,' she said and led the way to the counter.

Her bottom swung entrancingly in the jeans. It's a lousy idea, Teal told himself, and pulled his wallet out. She paid for the popcorn and he for two Cokes; they found their seats in the theater and almost immediately the lights dimmed. The film absorbed Julie instantly and she gave herself over to its intriguing tale. Fortunately Teal, like she, liked to sit through the credits at the end.

As they left the theater, she said inadequately, 'Well...I really need to talk about that. Want to go for a coffee?'

Her face was bemused, and her thoughts obviously not on him. 'Sure,' said Teal, and led the way to a little restaurant further down the mall.

Her observations were acute and more emotional than his; but she listened carefully to what he had to say, sometimes arguing, sometimes agreeing. He found himself liking her, and pushing the feeling down. He didn't want to like her; it would complicate his idea. While it was a very interesting idea, if he were sensible he'd go home and think about it before suggesting it to her.

As the waitress refilled their cups, he said abruptly, 'Julie, I've got a proposition for you.'

She glanced up, her smoke-blue eyes suddenly hostile. 'No, thanks. I get too many propositions—that's why I was going to the movies on my own.'

So much for liking her. 'I'm not Nick,' he rapped.

'Then don't behave like him!'

Teal wrapped his hands around his coffee-mug, trying to calm down. Why did he let her get under his skin so easily? Normally he thought of himself as an even-tempered man. 'I was using "proposition" in the legal sense,' he said. 'A plan, a project, a business undertaking. No sexual innuendoes. I hadn't realized how sensitive you were—I should have said I've got an idea.'

'I'm quite able to cope with words over two syllables, thank you! And I would have thought after what happened in the line-up that you might have understood my so-called sensitivity,' Julie rejoined, and watched his hand tighten around his mug.

Teal gulped down some coffee to give himself time to think. He hadn't even said what his idea was and already she was in a temper. Oh, well, he might as well go the whole hog. 'There's something I need to know first,' he said. 'Whether you're having an affair with Nick.'

'The worst womanizer in the hospital? You sure know how to pour on the flattery.'

'Yes or no will do,' Teal said, and something in his eyes caused hers to drop.

'No,' she said. 'I'm not into affairs. With Wayne or with Morse or with Nick.' Or with you, she added silently.

Teal wanted very badly to believe her. 'You mean you didn't go to bed with him after the dance?'

'Teal, what is this? You don't have the right to pry into my private life. I'm not asking if you've ever gone to bed with Deirdre Reid.'

'I haven't. She's into casual sex and I'm not.'

Somehow Teal's honesty seemed to call up an answering honesty in Julie—part of which was admitting to herself how glad she was that Teal wasn't involved with Dr Deirdre Reid. 'I did not go to bed with Nick the night of the dance,' she declaimed, 'I have never gone to bed with him, and I see no reason why I should ever want to.'

This time Teal believed her—and felt a strange lightness in his chest. Making a valiant effort to get back on track, he said, 'I'm not into affairs either, Julie, and I know I'm not explaining myself well. But I'm getting the impression that a lot of men are chasing you and you're not exactly delighted by that . . . am I right?'

'You couldn't be more right.'

'I spend a hell of a lot of energy keeping a bunch of women at bay who think I need a wife, a mother for Scott or a mistress on the side. You know what we should do?'

'No,' she said warily.

'We should join forces—start going out together. Get the word out that we're a couple. Then the men would leave you alone and the women would quit chasing me.'

He was smiling at her as though he'd solved all the world's problems. 'You're crazy,' she said.

'Think about it for a minute. Some guy puts the make on you . . . Sorry buddy, you can say, I'm already taken. A woman calls me up . . . No can do; I have a committed relationship with someone else.'

He was serious, she thought incredulously. 'I couldn't even begin to think of doing that.'

'Why not? And make it good.'

'Well, to start with, we scarcely know each other.'

'A couple of dates will fix that.'

'Oh, sure . . . in the most superficial way.'

'Superficial is what I'm talking about, Julie.' Warming to his idea, he added, 'Another thing each of us could do is write up a brief autobiography. Age, place of birth, names of sisters and brothers, that kind of thing. Just so we wouldn't disgrace ourselves when we're with other people.'

'We're not talking about applying for a passport,' Julie said, exasperated. 'This is about being a couple. About having a relationship.'

'Only in the outward sense. Only so that people will leave us alone.'

She was beginning to get his drift—and was not at all sure that she cared for it. 'We can't do it—we don't like each other,' she said triumphantly.

'All the better—this is a business arrangement. Sensible. Rational. The last thing we need is for feelings to get in the way.'

She remembered her first sight of him, standing in her kitchen in his pin-striped suit, unsmiling, critical, crushingly formal. Her nerves on edge, she said, 'I'm not sure you have any feelings.'

A muscle clenched in Teal's jaw. 'My feelings—or lack of them—are not what this is about. This is for convenience. So we can get on with the rest of our lives.' As the waitress brought the bill, he picked it up. 'I can see you don't like the idea. Let's just drop it, then. Do you need a drive home?'

He had given her a perfect opening to say goodnight and be on her way. She said curiously, 'How long would you propose this—this arrangement would last?'

'Until you decide you want another husband. Or I decide I want a wife.'

. 'For me, that could be a very long time,' Julie said; she heard the raw hurt underlying her words and could have bitten off her tongue.

'For me, too,' Teal said.

His lips were tight-held, his gaze turned inward. Impulsively she rested her hand on his. 'I shouldn't have said that about feelings—you've been hurt too, haven't you?'

He snatched his hand back. 'Let's get something straight. This game-plan of mine is just that—a game. On the surface, for appearances only. I don't want you prying into my life any more than you want me prying into yours.'

Her voice rising, she demanded, 'So what will we talk about when we're together? The weather? The day's headlines?'

Creasing the bill between his fingers, feeling his own temper rise that she could be so obdurate, Teal said, 'We wouldn't have to be together that much. Halifax is a small city where everyone's somebody else's cousin—it wouldn't take long to get the word around. We'd have to go to a few public places together and tell our friends and acquaintances that we're a couple. After that, we could relax. The occasional date would do it.'

Why was she even considering an arrangement so cold-blooded, so essentially deceitful? 'We couldn't possibly do this—what about the boys? They'd probably think we were going to get married.'

'Oh, we'd have to tell them the truth. Or a version of the truth. That we're friends and we're trying to make life a little easier for each other. They'd be fine with that. Scott hates it when my dates try and mother him.'

Danny had disliked Wayne on sight. 'What if either of us does meet someone else? Someone we do want to get involved with?'

'We'll end it. Simple.'

'It sounds so calculated,' she muttered. 'Utilitarian. Like we're a couple of robots.'

'It is calculated and utilitarian—that's the whole point. We're using each other to simplify our respective lives.'

She looked at him moodily. 'And what would the house rules be?'

'No prying into each other's past. No dating anyone else for the duration of the agreement.'

'What about sex?' she said bluntly.

Her fingernails were rhythmically tapping the plastic table and she looked about as friendly as Einstein the cat. Letting his anger show, Teal replied, 'This isn't just an elaborate ruse to get you into my bed.'

'You're the one who said I was loaded with sex appeal...how do I know I can trust you?'

Something approaching a smile lessened the tension in his face. 'You said the same of me.'

But for Julie this had gone beyond joking. 'Men take one look at me and think I'm up for grabs. Literally. But I'm not, Teal. I got so I hated sex in my marriage. The best thing it gave me was Danny, and the last thing I want is an affair. Is that clear?'

Her honesty, as always, exhilarated him. But he could in no way match it; the pain was too deep and he was too unused to speaking about his feelings. 'You'll be in no danger from me,' he said shortly.

The cold-eyed lawyer was very much in evidence. Julie said thoughtfully, 'Because you don't like me?'

'That's one reason,' Teal said, and was glad he wasn't under oath. 'The rest's none of your business.'

She should, perhaps, feel angry with him; she did not. 'I've got another rule,' she rejoined. 'Freedom to re-negotiate or end the arrangement at any time.'

'I think we should commit ourselves to at least three months,' he argued. 'Just to give it time to work.'

'That's the whole summer!'

The dismay on her face annoyed Teal immoderately. 'It's not a life sentence,' he said.

'It sounds like one—because we'd be acting the whole time. Pretending to be something we're not. I loathe falsity!' The words came out more vehemently than Julie had intended. But she couldn't retract them because they were true.

'Are your other dates any less false than our agreement would be?' As she winced, remembering the surgeon with the yacht, Teal said shrewdly, 'I thought not.'

She looked at him in silence. If she really hated falsity, why hadn't she left five minutes ago? Perhaps, under the skin, she was like all the other women: intrigued by Teal's paradoxical blend of magnetism and control.

'There's one more rule,' Teal said solemnly. 'No more than one container of buttered popcorn per day.'

'Each?' she quipped.

'Of course,' he said, and watched as a reluctant smile tilted her lips. 'Are we on, Julie?' he added, and held out his hand across the table.

'I must be crazy even to be considering it,' she said, keeping her hands in her lap.

'Am I that repugnant?'

'Don't fish for compliments,' she said trenchantly. 'You can get those from all your other women.'

'If you agree to this, I won't have any other women.'

Nor would she be dating men who seemed to think that the price of a meal was an invitation to maul her. Brightening, she said, 'I suppose we could look on it as a vacation.'

He was still holding out his hand. 'My arm's getting tired,' he said.

'I'm out of my mind,' Julie said, and shook his hand.

Her fingers were warm, with unexpected strength; he disliked weak handshakes. 'Good,' he said. 'I'll get a couple of tickets to the symphony benefit that's coming up next weekend—if you're free?' Julie nodded. 'That'll be a good start. Anything going on at the hospital?'

'There's a nurses' reunion at the end of the month; all the staff are invited,' she said faintly.

'Good. I'm adding another rule—you can't dance with Nick.'

'And I'm adding another one—that you can't keep adding to them.' She pushed back her chair. 'Come on, Teal—admit that we're crazy to be doing this.'

A smooth blonde curl had fallen free of its ribbon and was lying on the lightly tanned skin bared by the neckline of her shirt. He was quite sure she was oblivious of it. He said drily, 'A plea of temporary insanity? No way.'

'Huh,' she said, then looked down at her watch and yelped, 'Lord, is that the time? I told the sitter I'd be home ten minutes ago.'

'I'll take you to your car.'

'There's no need——'

'Someone got mugged in this parking lot last April. Don't argue.'

There was something in the set of his jaw that made Julie decide that arguing would be a definite waste of time. She hurried out of the mall, Teal at her side. When they got to her car, she unlocked the door, slid into her seat and said demurely, 'You're going to have your work cut out to make our first proper date as interesting as this one. Goodnight.'

'I'll do my best,' he said. 'And I'll call you tomorrow about the symphony. 'Night, Julie.'

His fingers were hooked in his belt, which was at eye level. 'I go to work at seven-thirty in the evening,' she mumbled, and backed her car out. One of the rules of this ridiculous game they'd agreed to play was no sex, and she had told the truth about her and Robert; why then were her palms damp and her mouth dry? And why was the thought of a symphony benefit filling her with such a complicated and unsettling mixture of excitement and dread?

Crazy. Insane. Deranged.

She was all three. She had to be to have agreed to Teal Carruthers' proposition.

CHAPTER FOUR

AFTER lunch on Monday Scott went to join Danny at the playground across the street. Teal had brought papers home from the office because Mrs Inkpen was on holiday, and headed for his study to work on his next case. He had phoned Julie yesterday to tell her he had two tickets to the symphony benefit. She had sounded very formal on the telephone; he had purposely not asked how she felt about their arrangement now that she'd had the chance to sleep on it. He'd have to remember to take his tuxedo to the drycleaners tomorrow.

He was absorbed in the complexities of the DNA evidence the police were presenting when he heard his son yell his name, a note in his voice that made Teal drop the sheaf of papers on the desk and take the stairs two at a time.

There were three people standing in his kitchen: Scott, Danny and a girl he had never seen before. Scott had dirt all over his face and a scrape on his chin, Danny had a black eye, a bloody nose and a cut lip, and the girl, who looked about fifteen, was crying. 'What happened?' Teal said economically.

'We were at the playground,' Scott burst out, 'and these kids from grade six were there; they picked a fight with us, and by the time Sally got there Danny had a black eye.'

'I'm Danny's sitter,' Sally sniffled. 'I was talking to my boyfriend and I didn't realize the boys were fighting. Mrs Ferris is going to be some mad at me.'

Teal knelt in front of Danny, assessing the damage. 'What was the fight about?'

'They said I was pretty,' Danny said, scowling ferociously and looking as far from tears as it was possible to look. 'They called me "pretty boy" and "mama's boy" and other stuff I didn't understand. They said stuff about Mum, too. So I punched one of them and then there was a big fight.'

'They were being very ignorant,' Teal said matter-of-factly, well able to imagine what the boys might have said and thinking it was just as well Danny hadn't understood it. 'I'll put some ice on your eye and your lip and wash your face, and you'll feel a whole lot better.'

'You gotta teach Danny how to fight,' Scott said excitedly. 'He doesn't know how.'

'I do so!' Danny said.

'I was fighting too, and I'm not all beat up like you,' Scott said unarguably.

'I punched the big guy real hard.'

'Okay, okay,' Teal interposed, hiding a smile as he tipped the contents of an ice tray on a clean towel. 'No point in starting another fight here in the kitchen. I could show you some useful defensive moves, Danny, that can keep you from being hurt, that's what Scott means...hold still now; this might sting.'

The damage was not as bad as it looked. But Teal made the boys sit down with milk and cookies after they were cleaned up, and directed Sally to the bathroom to wash her face. 'Where's your mother, Danny?' he said.

'Asleep. She worked last night and she goes to work again tonight. That's why Sally took me to the playground.'

As Sally came back in the room Teal said, 'I'll look after the boys for the rest of the day if you want to go home, Sally.'

But Sally had passed from tearfulness to a sense of duty. 'Mrs Ferris said I was to wake her up if anything happened,' she said righteously. 'So I'll have to take Danny home right now and tell her about the fight.'

'I'll go with you,' Teal said.

'Why, Dad?' Scott asked, big-eyed.

'To see if she wants me to give Danny some lessons in self-defense,' Teal answered promptly, and wondered if that was the only reason.

The stucco bungalow drowsed in the heat. But something was different, Teal thought, puzzled. The flowers, that was it. The garden was a patchwork of color, pinks and purples and reds and yellows in sprawling confusion. He found himself grinning without being sure why as he followed Sally in the back door.

Einstein, who was lying on the windowsill in the sun, gave him a dirty look. Same to you, thought Teal, still grinning, and realized he was intensely curious to see Julie again.

Sally disappeared. Then there was a flurry of footsteps on the stairs and Julie rushed in the kitchen. Her eyes flew to her son's battered face. 'Oh, Danny...sweetheart,' she said in a voice Teal had not heard her use before, and dropped to her knees in front of him.

Her hair was a glorious tangle around her face, and the silk floral robe she had wrapped around her body was already slipping, revealing a thin-strapped chemise in palest blue that clung to her breasts. 'What were you fighting for?' she gasped. 'You know I told you you mustn't fight. There's blood all over your shirt, Danny.'

'I got a real good punch in,' Danny said, speaking lop-sidedly because of his cut lip.

'I *hate* fighting,' his mother pronounced.

Teal cleared his throat. As Julie looked up he watched her eyes widen with shock. 'What are *you* doing here?' she demanded, scrambling to her feet with less than her usual grace and hastily tightening the belt of her robe.

'They came to my house first,' Teal said. 'It's closer to the playground. I put ice on his eye and his lip.'

'Oh,' said Julie. She felt fogged with tiredness, her lids heavy, her body craving sleep. She added belatedly, 'Thanks.'

'I also suggested he needs lessons in the art of self-defense.'

'That's the last thing he needs,' Julie said fractiously.

'You're not hearing me,' Teal replied with a blandness that irritated her out of all proportion. 'I said defense, not offense.'

'It's all fighting!'

'Scott was in the same fight and didn't get a black eye or a cut lip.' Teal quirked his brow. 'I rest my case.'

Why did she always feel at such a disadvantage with Teal? Julie wondered. Right now she was acutely aware that her gown barely skimmed her knees and that her first instinctive emotion on seeing him had been pure pleasure. Furious with herself as much as with him, she snapped, 'Why do men always think that a short course in violence will fix everything?'

Teal's mouth tightened. 'I'm not *men*—don't stereotype me. And I'm a lawyer, not a boxer. There's violence out there in the world, Julie Ferris; you know that as well as I do. I've never taught Scott to instigate it. But as a responsible parent I think it's my duty to equip him to deal with it. To protect himself when the need arises.'

Glancing down, he saw that their two sons were following every word. He said calmly, 'Sally, why don't you take the boys outside for a few minutes? Mrs Ferris and I need to discuss this in private.'

Sally gave him a bedazzled smile. 'Sure,' she said.

No sooner had the screen shut behind them than Julie fumed, 'You've got a nerve, giving my sitter orders in my own kitchen.'

Her cheeks were pale and her eyes blue-shadowed. Teal said, 'You look tired out.'

'Don't change the subject!'

She wasn't weeping, like Janine, and she certainly wasn't agreeing with every word he said, like Carole. She looked, if anything, ready to throttle him. He said casually, 'I'd like to take the boys home with me. I'm going to barbecue hamburgers around five—you could join us after you've slept again, and I'll show you what I've taught Scott. How about it, Julie?'

She looked him straight in the eye. 'What were they fighting about, do you know?'

It never occurred to him to fob her off with half-truths: this was a woman who wanted the whole truth and nothing but the truth. 'They called Danny a pretty boy and some other things that fortunately passed over his head... but I gather he didn't wade in with both fists flying until they insulted you.'

She ran her fingers through her hair, her shoulders slumped. 'Oh, damn,' she said.

Deliberately probing, Teal said, 'Maybe you'd rather Danny's father took him in hand as far as fighting's concerned?'

'He almost never sees him,' she said absently. She had withdrawn into herself, picking at a nick in the edge of the counter with her fingernail, her pose entirely unprovocative. But under the shiny pink roses on her robe he could see the agitated rise and fall of her breast and the curve of her hip; he was all too aware that they were alone in the house.

'Go back to bed,' he said harshly. 'I'll look after Danny, and you can come for supper at five.'

'I can't watch him all day,' she blurted with a touch of desperation. 'When I work nights, I have to get some sleep.'

'When I'm at the office or in court, I'm not with Scott—same thing, Julie.'

'You're telling me I shouldn't feel guilty, aren't you?' She sighed, crossing her arms over her breasts. 'I shouldn't, you're right. But I do. Anyway, there's no need for you to invite me and Danny for supper.'

'I already have.'

She gave him a hostile look. He was wearing navy sweatpants and a loose T-shirt, ordinary clothes that made her acutely conscious of the body beneath them. 'It's not in the agreement that we have meals together,' she announced. 'What's the point, after all? There's no one there to see us—unless the women who've been chasing you spy on your back garden with binoculars.'

Teal leaned against the counter, realizing that once again he was enjoying himself. 'You've got a mean tongue on you.'

'All the more reason for me to stay home.'

'The invitation has nothing to do with our agreement. I can show Danny a few moves and then we'll demonstrate what he's learned. I'm sure he'd love you to be there. After all, you are his mother.'

'A moment ago you said I shouldn't feel guilty and now you're trying to motivate me by guilt—do lawyers always play dirty?'

'Do I detect a certain prejudice against my profession?'

'Not prejudice. Outright dislike.'

He laughed and walked over to her. Julie held her ground, every nerve tense. Lifting her chin with one finger, he gave her a crooked smile. 'Go back to bed and set your alarm for quarter to five...I'll see you at five. I don't do desserts.'

'So it's my chocolate-fudge cookies you want, not me.'

'You got it.'

Teal dropped his hand to his side. Her skin was as silky as her robe, and she smelled faintly of flowers. But he didn't want her. Of course he didn't. That would be totally counter to their agreement. 'See you later—and lock the door behind me.'

Grimacing, Julie did as she was told. Crazy was exactly the word to describe her behavior as far as Teal Carruthers and his famous agreement were concerned.

Sharp at five Julie walked up the driveway of Teal's house. By following the delicious smell of roasting chicken, she located the gas barbecue on the back deck. The garden was a wild tangle of shrubbery and overgrown perennials that made her efforts in Mrs LeMarchant's garden look like those of a rank amateur. There was no one in sight.

She pushed open the patio doors and stepped inside, calling Teal's name. The room was large and airy, with off-white walls and a pale gray chesterfield set. The only pictures were black and white photographs, and the sole notes of color a couple of magazines lying on a glass coffee-table. Next time she came—if there was a next time—she'd bring a big bunch of petunias, she decided, standing near the hall door and stroking the undoubtedly expensive fabric on one of the wing chairs. Even a few nasturtiums would help.

From upstairs Danny gave a shriek of laughter, Scott yelled a warning, and footsteps hurtled down the stairs.

Before she could move, the door was thrust open and a body ran headlong into her. She was flung against the arm of the chair. The chair slid sideways across the carpet, dumping her flat on her back on the soft gray pile. A weight was crushing her chest, a weight that was warm and hard and smelled faintly of sweat. She looked up.

Teal's face was only inches from hers. He was naked to the waist, his body hair rough against her arm, the breadth of his shoulders blocking out the rest of the room. One of his knees had jammed itself between her thighs. The heat of his skin seeped through her cotton dress and burned into her palms, which were trapped against the corded muscles of his belly.

For a brief, searing moment she was thrown backwards in time to the early days of her marriage to Robert, when he had seemed to want her as much as she had wanted him, and when she had been happy. Deep within her, like an animal that had been long asleep, desire uncurled itself and stirred to life.

Teal lifted himself on his elbows and said flatly, 'God, Julie—did I hurt you?'

Making as much noise as a dozen small boys, Scott and Danny burst into the room, swinging on the door. 'What're you doing on the floor, Dad?' Scott asked with interest.

'Why's my mum underneath?' Danny added.

Hot color flooded Julie's cheeks. Bad enough that for a wild moment she had wanted to wrap her arms around Teal's neck and pull him back down to kiss her. Worse that their two sons should find them gazing into each other's eyes on the living-room carpet.

'I knocked her down,' Teal said in the same flat voice. 'By accident—I didn't know she was there. Are you okay, Julie?'

'I'm fine,' she muttered. It was a good thing she wasn't hooked to a lie detector; she was about as far from fine as she could be.

Then Teal got to his feet, taking her by the hands and pulling her up with him, so that she found herself standing entirely too close to a very impressive set of chest muscles. He was wearing the same navy sweatpants and nothing else. She yanked her hands free and said in a rush, 'I called your name but I guess you didn't hear me.'

A muscle was twitching in his jaw, and his gray eyes were as opaque as storm clouds. 'I'm sorry,' he said, 'really sorry...Scott, will you and Danny wipe off the picnic table while I check the barbecue?'

As the boys raced across the carpet and disappeared, Teal headed after them. His hair was tousled, his spine a long indentation from his nape to the elastic on his sweatpants, and he moved with a lithe grace. This time Julie's desire was not the gradual uncurling of an animal from its winter den, cautious and slow, but rather a great leap, like a tiger springing from its cage. A wild and unruly tiger, roaming free in search of its mate.

Shaken to the roots of her being, she stood still. And in her brain a small voice screamed, over and over again, No, no, no...

Dimly she heard the clatter of the barbecue tools as Teal turned the chicken on the rack. I've got to calm down, she thought frantically. I can't afford to feel like this. Not with Teal. Especially not with Teal.

Then the patio door slid open and he was standing in front of her again. Say something, Julie, she told herself. Act normally, as though nothing's happened.

He took her by the arm, his gray eyes full of concern. 'I hurt you, didn't I? You'd better sit down; you don't look so hot.'

His choice of words brought a bubble of hysterical laughter to Julie's lips. She choked it back. There was a dusting of dark hair over his breastbone, and a small white scar notched the curve of his topmost rib: intimate details that made her shiver with awareness. 'I'm all right,' she mumbled. 'You took me by surprise, that's all.'

And that's the truth, she thought, with another uprising of laughter.

Teal steered her over to the chesterfield and pushed her down on it. 'I'll pour you a drink. Stay put.'

She pulled the hem of her dress down over her knees. It was a pretty dress, with little flowers scattered over a thin cotton that molded her breasts and fell loosely to mid-calf. She should have worn something in heavy linen with long sleeves and a high collar, she thought, leaning her head back and closing her eyes. Like a nun's habit. Then a small body jumped on the chesterfield beside her, and Danny said, 'You all right, Mum?'

She smiled at him, rubbing her chin on the top of his head. 'Fine . . . how did you like your lessons?'

'Neat!' he crowed. 'Hey, Scott, come show my mum what we were doing.'

As the two boys started sparring in front of her, Teal came back in the room. After putting her drink on the coffee-table, he adjusted the set of Danny's shoulders, then demonstrated some fast footwork. Scott yelled encouragement. Teal jabbed a fist at him, Scott dodged with the ease of long practice, and suddenly all three of them were rolling around on the floor at her feet, Teal laughing breathlessly as the boys tried to tickle his ribs.

Julie clutched the glass to her chest, where a pain had lodged itself, sharp as a knife. Robert had never lost his dignity enough to fool around on the floor with his son. Never. As Danny butted his blond curls into Teal's armpit and Teal automatically put a protective arm around him, the pain spread. Danny needed what Teal was giving him. Needed it as much as he needed food and a roof over his head and his mother's love.

But this is only an arrangement between Teal and me, she thought numbly. An arrangement that might not last beyond three months. And then what?

She took a big gulp of rum and Coke, and followed it with another. Teal hauled himself upright, a boy clinging to each arm. His sweatpants had been dragged low over one hip; dark hair curled to his navel. Julie looked the other way and took another hefty swallow.

'The chicken must be ready by now,' Teal gasped. 'If you guys want to eat, you'd better treat the cook with more respect. Do you want to get the salad, Scott? And you could bring in the rolls, Danny.'

Danny gave him a gap-toothed grin. 'Sure,' he said, and raced after Scott.

'Bring your drink out on the deck, Julie,' Teal suggested, hitching at his waistband and trying to comb his hair into order. Then his gaze sharpened. 'What's wrong?'

'Nothing!'

He looked at her soberly, his gray eyes as clear as rainwater. 'I guess I've already come to count on your honesty—and that's not an honest answer.'

She stood up, tilting her chin. 'Our arrangement, you said, was to be superficial and convenient. Honesty and superficiality make strange bedfellows...you can't always have both.'

His lips compressed; he didn't like her reply one bit. 'Are you calling me a fool?'

'Myself, more likely,' she said, and deliberately changed the subject. 'How's the chicken? I'm starving.'

Although if I'm to be honest it's not for food, she thought, and strove to keep from blushing.

While he was sure something was wrong, Teal had no idea what it was. And it was pretty clear that Julie had no intention of telling him. He turned away, going out on the deck to check the barbecue one more time, sensing through every nerve-ending when she followed him. 'It's ready,' he said briefly. 'Pass me those plates, would you, Julie?'

They ate on a wooden picnic table on the deck, in the shade of an old maple tree that housed a family of chickadees. On the surface it was a light-hearted picnic. But all through the meal Julie was aware of Teal watching her, his expression inscrutable. She had no idea what he was thinking, and could only hope that he, equally, could not read her thoughts.

After they had eaten, the boys went inside to watch their favorite cartoon show on television. Julie sipped her coffee and said casually, 'Great flavour.'

'Java blend—I get it at the local delicatessen. We'll have to go there sometime; the owner's always trying to match me up with one of his four daughters.' He lifted his head. 'Now what are the boys squabbling about?'

Julie got up. 'I'll have to take Danny home soon anyway.'

She went inside, Teal close on her heels. The television was in a smaller room leading off the living-room. Even as she crossed the all too familiar gray carpet, she heard Danny say shrilly, 'He *is* my father!'

'Sure thing,' Scott replied with heavy sarcasm. 'Every kid on the block's got a father who's on TV.'

'He's an actor; that's why he's on TV!'

She pushed the door open, knowing what she was going to see, already hearing Robert's deep, beautifully modulated voice scrape across her nerves. A man and woman were sharing the screen, a tall, handsome man and a black-haired beauty; she stopped dead in her tracks. It was Robert. Robert and Melissa. Striving to sound natural, she said, 'That is Danny's father, Scott. His father and his stepmother.'

Danny, she saw, was on the verge of tears. She pulled him to her. 'I watched that play one night after you were in bed, Danny. Your dad won an award for it.'

'Robert Ferris,' Teal said quietly. 'I never made the connection.'

'No reason why you should,' Julie said coldly, rubbing at the tension in her son's shoulders.

'He's a fine actor.'

'Oh, yes,' she said, fighting to keep the irony from her voice, 'he's a very fine actor.'

Scott muttered, 'You're lucky, Danny—you got a famous father.'

Julie said steadily, 'There's a cost to being famous, Scott. You don't have a lot of time to spend at home, for instance. You don't have time for barbecues and teaching your son how to fight—because you're always off doing the things that make you famous.'

She could see Scott struggling to digest this, and from the corner of her eye saw Robert take Melissa in his arms and kiss her. Danny said, his voice quivering, 'Let's watch cartoons, Scott.'

'Okay,' said Scott. 'You can have my cars to play with while we watch.'

As Danny pulled free of his mother, Teal took her by the elbow. 'They'll be all right now,' he said. 'I'll pour you a fresh coffee.'

Julie didn't want coffee. She wanted to put her head down on the table and cry her eyes out. She shook her arm free and went back outside, the shadows from the leaves criss-crossing her face as she sat down.

'Teal,' she said abruptly, 'I can't go on with this arrangement of ours. I was silly even to consider it. I want to end it now before it really begins. Before we tell the boys.'

When he sat down across from her, the same shadows drifted lazily over his bare shoulders. She averted her eyes. He said evenly, 'Tell me what's going on.'

Oh, no, she thought, I'm not going to do that. 'I can't operate at a superficial level,' she said. 'We're not a lawyer and a witness in a courtroom, communicating in questions and answers. We're people, dammit! Living, breathing people. Or at least I am. Danny is. Scott is.' In a rush she finished, 'And I'm afraid Danny will get too fond of you if we keep on seeing each other.'

'This all started because Danny and Scott were friends,' Teal rejoined in a hard voice. 'If they're friends, Danny's going to be around me and Scott around you. That's got nothing to do with the two of us going out on a few dates, and you know it.'

'It's selfish and irresponsible.' She glared at him across the table. 'Only someone totally out of touch with his feelings could have come up with such a hare-brained scheme.'

'You seem to be forgetting that you agreed to it.'

'I've changed my mind.'

'A divorce before there's even been a wedding? So you're a quitter.'

'I'm not! I——'

'You're hyperventilating,' he said. 'Calm down.'

Her hiss of indrawn breath overrode the whispering of the leaves over their heads. Spacing her words, she said, 'I want out.'

'We said we'd give it a minimum of three months. This is less than forty-eight hours. We shook hands on it—it was a contract between us.'

'I didn't sign on the dotted line!'

His eyes narrowed. 'Why don't you tell me the truth about what's going on here?'

'I *am* afraid Danny will get too attached to you.'

'You can't legislate that,' Teal said forcibly. 'The same could be true of Scott—he already really likes you. Anyway, I know there's more to this than Scott and Danny. Come clean, Julie.'

'If I tell the truth, you'll think I'm just like the rest of them—all those women who are chasing you,' she said.

Then her eyes widened involuntarily. If she told the truth, he'd run a mile. Of course he would. He'd change his mind faster then Einstein could catch a rat. The beginnings of a smile on her lips, she said, 'All right—you asked for it. It's about sex.'

She had taken Teal by surprise, she could tell. 'You're too much man for me,' she went on crisply. 'When you were lying on top of me half naked, I wanted you to stay there.'

The wind moved softly through the trees and the birds chattered overhead. Teal sat still, his coffee untouched in front of him. Whatever he had expected, it had not been this. 'I don't believe you,' he said.

'You're overwhelming, you're gorgeous, you're sexy,' she answered with an impudent grin, feeling much better now that she had the problem out in the open. 'If you don't want me chasing you, you'd better end the agreement right now.'

He reached out and grasped her wrist with a strength that frightened her. 'Don't play games with me—I don't like it.'

Refusing to back down, she said, 'Some men might see the fact that I desire them as a compliment.'

'I'm not "some men"—I keep telling you that.'

Exasperated, she said, 'The rules specified no sex. So the agreement's over.'

'You're confusing the thought with the deed——'

'Oh, do stop talking like a lawyer!'

'I am a lawyer, and I'm damned if I'm going to spend half my time apologizing for that fact! You and I are not going to bed together, believe me. So there's no reason to end the agreement.'

Frowning, Julie said indelicately, 'Do you prefer men?'

'I do not. And I have a clean bill of health, in case that's what you're worrying about.'

'So you really don't have feelings.'

'Don't see me as a challenge, Julie—I won't put up with that.'

'Trying to get you to act like an ordinary man is not a challenge that interests me,' she seethed, and looked down at her watch. 'I've got to go. My shift starts at eight and I like to get there early.'

'Fine. I'm glad we had this discussion; it cleared the air—I now know you find me attractive and we both know we're not going to do anything about it. I'll see you Saturday at the symphony benefit. It's formal, by the way. And maybe one evening this week—say Thursday—we could exchange the autobiographies...that would probably save a lot of trouble.'

His face was expressionless and clearly he took her acquiescence for granted. As Julie felt her adrenaline level rise, she knew she hadn't been overly truthful a moment ago. She did see him as a challenge. Had done since he had first proposed the agreement. It would be exceedingly interesting to get beneath the surface of the man called Teal Carruthers and find out what made him tick.

She remembered his laughter as he'd rolled around on the floor with the boys. She remembered the bite of his fingers in her wrist and the cold anger in his voice. She remembered the heat of his body pressing her into the carpet.

Teal had feelings. She'd be willing to bet on it. What they were, and why he had buried them so deeply, was a mystery she might very easily want to solve.

Which could, of course, just be a different form of craziness.

CHAPTER FIVE

JULIE worked four straight night shifts that week, getting home from the last one on Thursday morning while Danny was still asleep. Because she now had four days off, she stayed up most of the day to get her sleeping patterns back on schedule.

Danny and Scott had both been invited to the same birthday party; when her son had gone, clutching his gift, Julie went out into the garden to do some weeding. The brigadier general was mowing his lawn ruthlessly short, a knotted handkerchief perched on his head. When he saw Julie, he turned off the mower and walked over to the fence. 'Your garden looks very nice,' he puffed, wiping his face. 'Ethelda will be pleased to see so many flowers.'

Ethelda was Mrs LeMarchant. 'Is she coming for a visit?'

'In two weeks,' he beamed. 'I'll be happy to see her, m'dear, I might as well tell you.' Checking that no one was in the vicinity, he leaned further over the fence and lowered his voice confidentially. 'You know, I once proposed to Ethelda—wasn't easy; I'd rather face an enemy battalion than ask a gel to marry me. She turned me down, though.' He gave a philosophical sigh. 'Just as well, I suppose. She never did approve of me going to the legion for a few beers—very strait-laced, Ethelda.'

Julie looked over the fence at his lawn, which was most certainly in apple-pie order. 'That's too bad,' she said. 'I would have thought you were soulmates.'

'We lived next door for nearly twenty years,' he answered wistfully. Then he straightened, tucking in his chin and clicking his heels together as best he could in his disgraceful old Oxfords. 'It's all for the best, no doubt. She didn't like me smoking a pipe, either—kept emptying the ashtray before I had the chance to fill it...ah, you have a guest, m'dear.'

Julie glanced over her shoulder. Teal was striding across the grass toward them. The autobiography, she thought in dismay. They'd agreed to get together tonight, and she'd forgotten all about it. Probably because she didn't want to do it. She smiled at him and quickly made the introductions. Teal put an arm around her shoulders, kissed her on the cheek and said, 'I missed you—seems like a long time since Monday.'

She gaped at him, wondering if he was out of his mind. His lips had been warm on her cheek and the weight of his arm felt altogether wonderful. Then, in peculiar mingling of relief and disappointment, she realized what he was doing. He was giving the general the message that she was taken: the agreement put into action. In swift mischief she laced her arms around his waist and batted her lashes at him. 'I missed you too,' she said.

'Hrrumph,' said the general. 'Must get back to my lawn, m'dear. Good evening to you, Mr Carruthers.'

Under the roar of the mower Teal said, 'Took you a while to catch on.'

'Give me a break—I've been on my feet for twenty-eight hours. And no, I don't have my autobiography done; I forgot all about it.'

Looping his arm around her waist, Teal steered her back to the house. 'Let's go inside; I can't hear myself think with that noise.'

His hip moved against hers as they walked, and she could feel the heat of his arm through her thin cotton shirt. The tiger called desire ripped at her composure and, irritably, as soon as they were out of sight of the general, she pulled free. 'I don't know if I'm up for this; I'm really tired.'

'It won't take long,' Teal said implacably. 'Just a few facts.'

The kitchen was cool, Einstein sprawled belly up on the tiled floor. Julie poured two glasses of iced tea, added slices of lemon and took the sheet of paper Teal was holding out to her. It was a computer printout, which for some reason incensed her. She plunked herself down on one of the stools and tossed the paper on the counter. 'Why don't you just tell me what's in it?'

Teal sat down as well, crunching a piece of ice between his teeth. Her legs—those impossibly long legs— were tanned a light golden colour; she had shucked off her sandals when she had come in the door, and the mud between her toes filled him when an emotion he could not possibly have categorized.

He said, 'I'm thirty-four years old, born in Ontario, an only child. My parents divorced when I was six and had joint custody. I left home—or I suppose I should say homes—when I was seventeen and graduated from law school when I was twenty-four. I was asked to join a top Toronto firm, where I discovered I hated corporate law, and shortly afterwards met Elizabeth. We married, moved to Halifax, and had Scott.' He paused. 'She died two years ago. The rest you know.'

Julie poked at the ice cubes in her glass. They bobbed on the surface with most of their volume hidden, rather like Teal's recital of facts. 'Joint custody was unusual thirty years ago, wasn't it?'

'My parents had never been able to agree on anything. No reason why they should agree on who had custody.'

She licked her finger, then flicked a glance at Teal. 'They both wanted you that much.'

In spite of himself his mouth tightened. 'Yeah,' he said.

'You're lying, Teal.'

He forced himself to calmness. 'Those facts should be all you'll need. I have a couple of cousins in Ontario whom I see occasionally, and I was a champion sculler and chess player at university.'

Both solitary pursuits, she thought, unsurprised. Although the sculling would explain his chest muscles. She said, trusting her intuition, 'Neither of your parents wanted you, did they?'

With brutal force Teal answered, 'Lay off, Julie. This agreement isn't about mutual psychoanalysis and I'll thank you to keep——'

'Everything superficial,' she flashed. 'It's not your fault if your parents didn't want you.'

'——your nose out of my business,' Teal finished with deadly precision. 'Now it's your turn. How old are you? Where were your born?'

'I'll tell you one fact,' Julie said tightly. 'In all my twenty-eight years I have never met a man who makes me as angry as you do.'

His smile was full of mockery. 'That's two facts.'

She got up from her stool, her arms crossed over her chest, and prowled up and down the kitchen, clipping off her words. 'Born on a farm in New Brunswick, parents still living, two older sisters, met Robert while doing my nurses' training in Halifax, married at nineteen, lived on the south shore, had Danny, divorced seven months ago and moved to Halifax. I hope you took notes because I'm not going through it again.'

'And you hated sex.'

'That's not the kind of fact you need. You've got what you need. Goodbye, Teal,' she snapped.

She looked as though she would take considerable pleasure in pouring the jug of iced tea over his head. Mingled with his anger, laughter bubbled in his chest. Knowing that if he were wise he'd head for the door, Teal asked with genuine interest, 'Monday night you said you wanted to go to bed with me—how can you desire someone you don't even like?'

'At the moment my one desire is for you to leave my house!'

He stood up, his muscles uncoiling with easy strength, and for an exhilarating moment forgot logic and caution. One thing was crystal-clear to him: he was not about to obey her. Paraphrasing what she had told him, he said, 'In all my thirty-four years I have never met a woman as beautiful as you.'

He had expected her to blush, or at least look confused. Instead she looked around the kitchen, her brows raised, and remarked, 'Apart from Einstein—who is manifestly uninterested in us—we're quite alone. So if I were you, Teal, I'd save the compliments for the symphony benefit, when we'll have an audience who'll appreciate your winning way with words.'

How long was it since a woman had made him laugh? Too long, Teal thought, and walked closer to her, watching unease dart across her face. 'I need practice,' he drawled.

'Sing my praises in the shower,' she retorted. 'Proclaim my virtues to the mirror when you're shaving. But right now go home.'

Suddenly for Teal the game changed into something very different. Different and far more dangerous. He said, 'That isn't what I need to practise. And I don't like being told what to do.'

'Of course not—because you're into control,' she rejoined. 'Controlling everyone, including yourself. Yourself worst of all.'

'When I want your diagnosis I'll ask for it,' Teal snarled, taking her by the elbows and pulling her toward him. She was taller than Elizabeth and fitted into his arms as if she had been made for him, her breasts brushing his chest with tantalizing softness. Before she had time to react, he took her chin in one hand, lowered his head and kissed her full on the mouth.

He had begun this from some primitive need to assert himself, to let Julie know she couldn't get away with telling him what to do—and found that the warmth of her mouth and the startled rigidity of her body made him instantly lose the very control she had accused him of. His senses swimming, he buried one hand in the silken weight of her hair, caressed the long curve of her waist and hip with the other, and deepened the pressure of his lips on hers.

He wanted her to respond. With every cell in his body he wanted to know that he had that power over her, the most basic power in the world.

And suddenly, to his infinite gratification, she yielded to him, her arms looping around his neck, her lips parting. Dizzy with the sweetness of her mouth and the pliancy of her body, he thrust with his tongue, cupping her face in his palms and kissing her as if there were no tomorrow. Only now. A man and a woman meeting as though for the first time, in that place where nothing else mattered but the beat of blood and the imperious heat of desire.

He wanted her. Wanted her now. Wanted her in——
And here Teal's thoughts stopped short and with agonizing swiftness he plummeted into that cold place of despair where Elizabeth's death had left him. Fool, he

thought savagely. You fool...are you going to let yourself be caught again? Is that what you want?

He pushed Julie away, hearing his breathing rasp in his throat, seeing blank shock obliterate the blur of passion in her smoke-blue irises. 'I shouldn't have done that,' he grated. 'It won't happen again, I swear it won't.'

She staggered a little, grabbing at the counter for support, and even in the midst of a turmoil that was tearing him apart Teal was aware of admiration as he watched her struggle to find words. 'That wasn't practice,' she managed finally. 'That was the real thing.'

She was wrong. Utterly and completely wrong. 'No, it wasn't,' he said offensively. 'It's what happens when I don't take the Deirdre Reids of this world to bed.'

Julie flinched visibly. Her hand made a tiny, telling gesture of distress as she said, 'It's me, isn't it? It happens all the time. There's something about me—my looks, my body—that drives men crazy. But it's nothing to do with the real me. The person under the face, the woman under the skin. None of you is the slightest bit interested in her.'

To Teal's horror her lip was trembling. She turned away, pulled a tissue from the box on the counter and noisily blew her nose. In a cracked voice he said, 'I haven't gone to bed with anyone since Elizabeth died.'

Julie spun round, her eyes awash with unshed tears. '*What* did you say?'

Wishing the words unsaid, Teal muttered, 'You heard—and now I'm getting the hell out of here. I'll pick you up at seven-thirty on Saturday.'

'You must have loved her very much.'

He couldn't take any more of this. 'I'll see you Saturday,' he repeated, brushed past her and took the back steps two at a time in his haste to be gone. As he jogged down the street towards his house, finding relief in physical action, he knew he'd learned one thing in the last ten minutes. He wouldn't ever kiss Julie Ferris again.

Not for a thousand agreements would he do that.

Saturday night found Julie in a horrible state of nerves. On Thursday in the kitchen she had decided that Teal was just like all the other men who had passed through her life in the last few weeks, interested only in her appearance and her body, kissing her out of lust and that deadly male drive for power. But then, like a knife in her heart, she would remember the anguish in his gray eyes as he had confessed to her that his bed had been empty for two long years.

He hadn't meant to tell her that, she would swear to it.

Why had he been celibate since Elizabeth's death?

The obvious answer was the one she had instinctively spoken: that he had loved his wife so much he couldn't bear to replace her with anyone else. But Julie wasn't sure that was the real—or the only—answer. Somehow, she mused, smoothing on pink lipstick with absent-minded care, it all came down to that word control. Teal had his emotions so deeply buried it would take an earthquake to free them.

Or a kiss, she thought wryly. A kiss that for her had been the equivalent of an earthquake.

And, of course, it was her ambivalence toward Teal that had caused her yesterday to commit herself to being with him for the next three months, accepting the challenge of a man who excited, infuriated and mystified her.

Last night she had taken Danny aside and explained what she privately called The Agreement to him, knowing it was a fateful step yet finding to her chagrin that he was only a touch more interested than Einstein would have been. 'That's neat—can I go out and play for another half an hour, Mum?' he had said, and all her carefully rehearsed justifications had remained unsaid.

Ten minutes before Teal was to pick her up, Julie was ready. In silence she looked at herself in the mirror in her bedroom. She had had two dresses to choose from for her début as Teal's partner—a pretty full-length dress with a swirling skirt of many colors, and the one she was now wearing.

My minimalist period, she thought, dry-mouthed, tossing her head so that her earrings caught the light and admitted to herself that she was using the most basic of weapons to attack Teal's control. The dress was covered in glossy pearl-white sequins; it bared her throat, her cleavage, her shoulders and arms, most of her back and, from mid-thigh, her legs. Pearlized pantihose and thin-heeled pumps completed her outfit.

She would be noticed, that was for sure.

The outer woman was firmly in place, she thought, staring at her reflection. The surface woman, beautiful and assured, whom men wanted to bed and whom a lot of women disliked.

Panic-stricken, she ran for her closet and pulled out the other dress, fumbling for the zipper on the back of the one she was wearing. Downstairs the doorbell pealed. Her hands stilled. Teal was early. She would have to keep on the dress she had chosen.

She shot herself a hunted glance in the mirror. This was all about acting, wasn't it? And after all, what was she complaining about? The dress was a knockout, she loved to dance and she was dating the sexiest man in the city. If not the entire province.

She ran downstairs and pulled the front door open, standing back so Teal could come in, her eyes lowered in sudden shyness. The evening sun shone full on her, glinting among the sequins and shimmering in the loose fall of her hair. Teal stood stock-still on the step. 'My God,' he said.

Her strategy had worked. So far at least.

Her lashes flickered upward. He looked magnificent in a tuxedo, his pleated shirt-front a crisp white, his height and breadth of shoulder subtly emphasized by the formality of his attire. She managed a weak smile. 'I echo your sentiments exactly.'

Fighting to recover his composure, Teal said brusquely, 'Are you ready?'

'My shawl's in the kitchen.'

She led the way down the hall, achingly conscious of him following her. As she reached for the lacy shawl hanging on the back of one of the stools, he passed her a small white florist's box. 'I'm not sure there's enough dress to pin them on,' he said drily.

She took the box with noticeable reluctance, opening it slowly. Nestled in tissue paper was a corsage of two exquisite pale pink orchids. She blurted, 'Why did you do that? You didn't have to,' and winced at her own lack of finesse.

'Don't you like orchids?'

'They're beautiful,' she said truthfully. 'But...'

'But what, Julie?'

She raised her chin. 'Robert didn't believe in giving gifts. But just about every man I've dated in the last three months has given me a gift of some kind. A gift with a price attached that's supposed to make me feel grateful and indebted so later on I'll come across.'

'Sexually.'

'Well, of course.'

His gray eyes were opaque with anger. 'I said on Thursday I wouldn't touch you like that again and I meant it.'

She could feel tears pricking at the backs of her eyes. 'So why are you giving me orchids, Teal?'

'They're a gift. Unentailed. Freely given. If you can't accept them in that spirit, you can throw them on the compost heap for all I care!'

She said carefully, 'I don't understand... you just felt like giving them to me?'

His fury vanished as quickly as it had arisen. 'This is a big deal for you, isn't it?'

'Pretty big, yes.'

'If I say they were so beautiful that they reminded me of you, you'll jump on me,' he said with a twist of his mouth. 'But that was one reason.'

'What were the others?'

He jammed his hands deep in his trouser pockets. 'I suppose because I admire your honesty and courage.'

The waxen petals of the orchids blurred in Julie's vision. 'If I start to cry,' she said shakily, 'it'll ruin my mascara and then we'll be late.'

Unable to prevent himself, Teal stepped closer. 'Didn't your husband love you?'

She shook her head. 'He only loved himself. I was a useful ornament, a tribute to his good taste, to be trotted out on appropriate occasions. The terrible thing is that I don't think he ever loved Danny, either.'

'The man's a fool. You know that?'

She gave a helpless shrug. 'We'd better go.'

Very gently Teal rested his hands on her bare shoulders. 'So what's to be the fate of the orchids? Your dress or the compost pile?'

She looked up, aware of the slight roughness of his palms in every nerve in her body, and said without artifice, 'I'd be proud to wear them.' Her mouth quirked. 'But I think you'll have to pin them in my hair; there's no room on the dress.'

His eyes ranging her face, Teal said roughly, 'Every time I go near you, things go awry. I figured you'd be pleased to be given orchids, you'd thank me, and that would be that. In my experience most women accept gifts as their due, one of the pleasantries that go with dating.'

She tossed her head. 'You didn't give me orchids because I'm superficial.'

'Are you ever at a loss for an answer?'

'With you, I'm not sure I even know the question.'

He gave an impatient sigh. 'The orchids, Julie.'

She pulled a comb that was glittering with rhinestones out of her hair. 'Can we attach them to that?' she asked, and watched as he did so with deft fingers. Then he reached over and pushed the comb back into the thick waves of her hair.

His voice taut with repressed feeling, he said, 'You could have stepped out of a Gauguin painting. You look exotic...pagan.'

With no idea where the words came from Julie whispered, 'Please don't hate me, Teal.'

'I have no more intention of hating you than I have of loving you,' he said levelly. 'This arrangement is for our mutual convenience, and if we don't leave soon we'll be late for dinner.'

He had withdrawn to a place she couldn't follow; nor was it the first time he had done that. Feeling her insides churn with nervousness, Julie said, 'Wait here a minute.' Then she took a pair of scissors out of the drawer and hurried outside. Within two minutes she was back, carrying a pale pink rosebud from the garden, the petals smooth as silk and delicately scented. Rummaging in the same drawer, she came up with a safety-pin. 'Hold still,' she ordered, and took the lapel of his jacket in her fingers.

Teal, who hated being controlled, stood still. In his nostrils Julie's scent mingled with that of the rose as she wrestled with the safety-pin and the thorns on the stem, her tongue caught between her teeth as she concentrated on her task. Her skin, he was sure, would be as smooth as the petals of the rose, and her beauty was every bit as complex. What would it be like to watch her unfold to him, open like a rosebud to the sun?

His heart was hammering in his chest so loudly that he wondered if she could hear it. She gave a tiny exclamation of pain as she stabbed herself on a thorn, then finally managed to secure the rose at the angle she wanted. 'There,' she said with immense satisfaction, stepping back and smiling at him.

She wasn't flirting with him, and he knew that what she had done was somehow very important to her. 'Did you give gifts to Robert?' he asked.

With painful accuracy she said, 'I used to at first. But then I'd discover them lying around broken or uncared for, and realized he didn't want them or value them. So I stopped.' She bit her lip. 'He didn't even notice that I'd stopped—I think that was what hurt the most.'

He remembered how she had stood in front of the television set in his house, holding her son to her body as she watched her ex-husband and his second wife kiss each other on the screen; and how all her normal vitality and joy of life had drained out of her, leaving her looking depleted and tired, older than her years. The words wrenched from him, he said, 'Do you still love him?'

She shook her head. 'No... the day he told me he was divorcing me for Melissa I realized that I'd stopped loving him quite a while ago. It was humiliating and horrible to be told there was another woman, and I was

furious at the way he'd deceived me. But even though
my self-esteem was at an all-time low, my heart wasn't
broken.' She sighed. 'Yet when we got married I was
crazy about him.'

Teal had been in love with Elizabeth on his wedding-
day. But why was he even thinking about Elizabeth? And
why was he asking Julie about her husband when he
would refuse outright to answer similar questions about
his wife? He said, feeling gauche and off balance and
masking it with a surface politeness, 'Thank you for the
rose, Julie . . . and now we'd really better go.'

Politeness could be deadly, Julie thought, already regretting her confidences. Rather than thanking her, Teal
might just as well have slammed a metal fence between
them plastered with 'No Trespassing' signs: it would have
been more honest.

But then the agreement wasn't about honesty. It was
about superficiality.

She picked up her shawl, draping it round her
shoulders, and walked out to the car with him.

CHAPTER SIX

JULIE had cheered up by the time she and Teal arrived at the hotel, and was wickedly amused that almost the first couple they met when they entered the big ballroom was Nick accompanied by Deirdre. You two deserve each other, she thought. And this is where I get some fun out of The Agreement. She tucked her hand in the crook of Teal's elbow and said demurely, 'Good evening, Nick . . . Dr Reid.'

Nick raised one brow in a way she was sure most women found irresistible. 'I didn't know you two were dating each other.'

'Come on, Nick,' she teased. 'Teal and I were made for each other—or so we've discovered, haven't we, darling?' And she laughed up at her companion, leaning her cheek intimately against his black-clad shoulder.

Only she felt the steel-hard tension in his arm and the tightness in his shoulder muscles as Teal said with a perfect blend of warmth and conviction, 'Absolutely . . . a match made in heaven.'

'A match that must have happened very fast,' Nick said quizzically.

'Just like lightning,' Julie rejoined. 'That's how we knew it was so right for us.'

'So I don't even get one dance?' Nick queried.

'Oh, maybe one,' Julie said.

'Only one,' Teal announced with an unarguable ring of authority.

Deirdre said sweetly, 'Really, Teal, you're the last man I would have expected to fall for a pretty face.'

'Life is full of surprises, Deirdre,' Teal said with a blandness that amused Julie mightily. 'Although "pretty" is a gross understatement.'

As he looked down at Julie, even she, knowing he was acting, was disarmed by the glow in his eyes. He added, 'We'd better go in search of Bruce and Marylee, Julie; they're holding a place for us.'

Julie gave the other couple a dazzling smile that she hoped was untinged with malice, and allowed Teal to steer her among the circular dinner-tables, which were decorated with flowers and sparkling silverware. Teal growled in her ear, 'One of our rules was that you couldn't dance with Nick.'

She said with impeccable logic, 'We need Nick to get the message you and I are a number—he knows so many women that that should ensure your safety.'

'You have a point. Just don't let his hands go any lower than your waistline.'

Tucking in the back of her mind the knowledge that Teal had noticed Nick's roaming fingers, Julie replied with exaggerated complaisance, 'Your every wish is my command.'

Teal gave a reluctant chuckle. 'Spare me, Julie—I know you better than that.'

She widened her eyes and pouted her lips. 'But this is about acting, Teal, not about reality.'

Once again, Teal thought, she had gotten under his skin. 'I hadn't forgotten,' he said smoothly. 'You can trust me to impress upon your favorite female surgeon that you and I are meant for each other—which should get the word around the hospital. Now come and meet my best friends.'

Julie liked Marylee and Bruce immediately, and did her best to act like a woman smitten. It was uphill work, partly because she felt she was being deceptive with a couple who clearly cared for Teal, partly because Teal all of a sudden was giving her very little help. With his innate good manners he made sure she was included in every conversation, filling her in on private and long-held jokes among the other three. But if he was trying to give the impression of a man madly in love he was out to lunch. Or, more appropriately, out to dinner.

The remains of an excellent lobster cocktail were removed, and the band was playing a waltz. Julie rested her fingers on Teal's wrist. 'Dance with me, darling? I love to waltz.'

Teal didn't know which he hated most: his body's instant response to her touch, or the fraudulence behind her endearment. 'Sure,' he said, getting to his feet and taking her by the hand.

The dance-floor was parquet, large and dimly lit. As Teal took Julie in his arms, holding her an impersonal distance from his body, she said in a furious whisper, 'You're not behaving at all like a man in love... what's wrong with you? I feel like an idiot, lacing my conversation with "darling"s and "honey"s—I never realized how much I dislike that word honey—and falling all over you while you sit there like a stick talking to Bruce about the scarcity of brook trout.'

Teal missed a step. 'Sorry,' he muttered. 'Did I forget to tell you? I warned Bruce and Marylee what was going on—so there's no need to pretend in front of them.'

'You mean I've been acting my fool head off for nothing?' Julie squeaked.

'They're my best friends; I couldn't deceive them. I told them about our agreement a couple of days ago.'

'Thanks a lot,' she said bitterly. 'I only hope Nick isn't watching us have our first fight—that man's got eyes in the back of his head. Teal, we can't turn it on and off like a tap. Either we're in love or we're not.'

Angry with himself, he said shortly, 'I should have told you—I'm sorry.'

'I feel like I've made a fool of myself!'

'Look on it as practice for when you dance with Nick.'

'To hell with Nick—this is about us.'

He said in a measured voice. 'Nick and Deirdre have just joined us on the dance-floor—smile, Julie.'

She directed a ferocious smile at him and said through gritted teeth, 'Is there such a thing in your law books as justifiable homicide? If so, it might be wise of you to check your soup for arsenic.'

Laughing, Teal led her through an intricate *chassé*. 'They've delivered the salad to our table; we could sit down now... and I think you should drop calling me honey; I don't like it, either.'

'What I feel like calling you at this precise moment is unprintable,' Julie said, waving in a sprightly fashion at Nick and Deirdre, and then wending her way back through the tables to the one they were sharing with Bruce and Marylee.

It was a Caesar salad, which Julie adored, followed by Chateaubriand and strawberry cheesecake; throughout the rest of the meal Julie did not once touch Teal and called him neither darling nor honey. Then, as liqueurs and coffee were poured, the band struck up again. Bruce swung Marylee up on the dance-floor, and more sedately Teal followed suit.

While Julie also danced with Bruce and a couple of Teal's colleagues as the evening went on, she mostly danced with Teal. She could not fault his technique, for he knew steps she had never even thought of and guided her through them with a skill she had to admire. But, although he held her close enough to satisfy the impression they were trying to give of two newly met lovers, his body was taut with an underlying resistance, and he danced as if the music never once touched his soul.

Julie had loved to dance for as long as she could remember; losing herself in music's rhythms and surrendering to its melodies had always freed her from the cares of every day. But Teal was surrendering nothing. At midnight, as she circled the floor with him, she found herself thinking, I hate this. It's all an act, and I hate it. I can't stand the way he's so controlled.

While she was getting dressed earlier this evening she had worried that she'd be ravaged by desire for Teal in the middle of the dance-floor. She needn't have worried, she thought grimly. Dancing with Teal was more of an ordeal than an incentive to lovemaking.

Not stopping to think, she said, 'You know how bananas get when they're overripe—sort of mottled and squishy? Do you like them like that?'

Puzzled, Teal said, 'Can't say that I do.'

'That's the way you're holding me. As if I were an overripe banana.' Warming to her theme, she added, 'Or something rather disgusting that's been tucked at the back of your refrigerator, all green and slimy and long overdue for the garbage can. You know the kind of thing I mean? You pick it up in the very tips of your fingers.'

As the waltz ended, Teal whirled her in a complicated turn. 'You don't like the way I dance?' he said coldly.

Over her shoulder she saw Nick leading Deirdre in their direction. She smiled provocatively at Teal, running her fingernail down the nape of his neck, and said, just as the band launched into some raucous rock and roll, 'You're extremely competent—and here comes Nick.'

'Dance, Julie?' Nick asked.

'Love to,' she said promptly.

The beat of the bass pulsed through her veins, and in a surge of rebellion Julie forgot that she was supposed to be the love of Teal's life and for the first time that night danced her heart out, a lithe, sexy figure in her spangled dress. Nick caught the wildness of her energy, and when the song came to an end there was a brief smatter of applause. In faint dismay Julie looked around for Teal. He was standing at the edge of the floor talking to Deirdre. 'I promised Teal this one, Nick,' she lied valiantly.

As Teal watched her walk back toward him, he was so overwhelmed by primitive aggression that part of him—but only a very small part—was horrified. By a huge effort of will he managed to wait until Deirdre and Nick had joined another couple before seizing Julie by the elbow and marching her to a secluded corner behind some large, anemic-looking potted palms. Pulling her round to face him, he blazed, 'You did sleep with him, didn't you?'

'I did not!'

'Don't lie to me—I watched the two of you on the dance-floor and I know basic chemistry when I see it.'

It had been a very long evening, and Julie was tired of pretending to be something she was not with someone who couldn't stand even to hold her in his arms.

'I'm not sexually attracted to Nick and never have been,' she flared. 'I told you that the night we began this ridiculous agreement. Your problem is that you don't recognize basic chemistry when it's standing right under your nose!'

'And what's that supposed to mean?'

A palm branch was gently waving over his head, but she had no inclination to laugh; he looked far too angry for that. Nor had she meant to speak her mind quite so forthrightly. Equivocating, she said, 'You already know that I find you attractive.'

'That is not what you meant!'

'All right, it's not! When you kissed me in the kitchen the other evening I felt as though the sun, the moon and the stars had all come out at once. But did you recognize that? Oh, no—you pushed me away as though you'd been embracing a piece of poison ivy and then you apologized all over the place. That's what I mean.'

Spacing his words, Teal said, 'I don't want to get sexually involved with anyone, Julie Ferris, and that includes you. Have you got that straight?'

'So why should you care whether I slept with Nick?'

'The guy's a lush.'

'Whereas you're a monk.'

He said unpleasantly, 'If this were one of your husband's plays, I'd now haul you off to bed to prove my manhood. You've got the wrong plot—and the wrong man. You can't provoke me into doing something I don't want to do.'

'So what's so awful about sex, Teal?'

She had asked the one question he couldn't possibly answer.

'Why would I want to have sex with a woman who hates it?' he said meanly, and watched her flinch.

'I'll never in a million years dance with Nick again,' she said bitterly. 'But if you want this agreement to succeed, you and I have got to stop dancing like a couple of strangers—or no one's going to believe that we're in love.'

'Bruce has already told me more or less the same thing.'

Bruce, in less colorful language than Julie's, had claimed that Teal was holding Julie like a maiden aunt.

Julie sighed, suddenly feeling extraordinarily tired. 'I don't understand you at all,' she muttered. 'I've never met anyone who kept his emotions and his sexuality so much under wraps.'

'You don't have to understand me! This is an arrangement for our mutual convenience—and that's all it is.'

Her shoulders slumped. 'I don't think it'll work. Because it's a toss-up which of us is the worse actor.'

Teal raked his fingers through his hair and said with raw honesty, 'Certainly superficiality flies out of the window whenever we come within ten feet of each other.'

She grinned ruefully. 'You've noticed that?'

'Yeah, I've noticed it . . . I'm not that much out of touch.' He hesitated. 'You look wiped—why don't we have one more dance and then leave?'

'It's hard work, pretending to be in love. Maybe we should have put an announcement in the paper and skipped the public performances.'

Through the potted palms 'Lara's Theme' drifted to Teal's ears; it was one of his favorite songs. 'I love that music,' he said. Suddenly sick to death of play-acting, he lifted her hand to his lips. 'Dance with me, Julie?'

There was no one else in sight; his gesture had been for her alone. Her heart playing its own melody in her breast, a wild and happy little melody, Julie said, 'Thank you, I'd like that.'

Teal took her hand in his, cradling it, and led her back to the dance-floor. This time when he took her in his arms he didn't send out any mixed messages; his arms strong around her, he drew her close and left out all his fancy steps, his cheek resting on her hair as he swayed to the music. Julie dropped her head to his shoulder, closed her eyes and let the hauntingly sad tune envelop her. For the first time in several hours she felt happy—as though she was where she wanted to be.

Slowly and lazily the tiger uncoiled itself, stretching its sleek limbs in indolent pleasure. Julie watched it in her mind's eye, held Teal a little closer and let her senses take over. His body was hard and fit, his strength understated, while his skin smelled of soap and shaving lotion and something both more individual and more elusive that was the very essence of the man. She let one hand drift to the back of his neck and moved a little closer to him, so that her breasts were pressed to his chest.

Then, with a thrill of sheer pleasure, she felt his hand slide across the bare expanse of her back, pulling her closer still. They were dancing hip to hip; there was no mistaking his arousal. No mistaking, either, the fact that he hadn't tried to hide it from her.

She wanted Teal; wanted him so badly she was almost faint with longing. She wanted to be intimate with him in ways she could barely imagine, ways that made her heartbeat race and the blood sing in her veins. What she had learned in the last few minutes was that he wanted her, too.

As Lara's song came to an end, Teal muttered, 'I can recognize body chemistry when it's under my nose.'

She said contentedly, 'So can I.'

With a little edge to his voice he said, 'I didn't want you thinking I was in any way defective.'

She suddenly reared her head, as alert as a wild animal at the first scent of danger. 'That wasn't just a game for you, Teal?' she said, appalled.

He countered that with another question. 'Do you still have complaints about my dancing?'

'No. Answer me!'

He couldn't; he didn't know what to tell her. He said coolly, 'Then let's say goodbye to Marylee and Bruce and I'll take you home.'

Julie didn't want to go home; she wanted to stay in an embrace that had filled her with a dizzying mixture of security and desire. Openly pleading with him, she said, 'The way we danced—that was real! For me it was real. Wasn't it for you?'

'You know what the agreement said—no sex.'

He was easing her away from his body. In true anguish she said, 'I have to know when we're acting and when we're not—I have to!'

He said hoarsely, 'I might live like a monk. That doesn't mean I don't have the normal urges of a man. I'd have to be two years old or a hundred and two not to want you, Julie—but that doesn't mean I'm going to do anything about it.'

It was not the answer she had hoped for, but it was all the answer she was going to get. He hadn't had a woman in two years; and she, Julie, had thrust herself at him, flaunting her body in a dress that left little to the imagination, constantly needling him. Of course he was aroused. A stone statue would have been aroused.

And once again she had exposed her feelings to him, her vulnerabilities. She was as transparent as a piece of glass, she thought wretchedly. Whereas he was like a mirror, reflecting the enigma of the man himself and nothing more.

With a sudden need to revenge herself, she curved her lips in a seductive smile, brushed her breasts lightly against the front of his jacket and said, 'You've never made love on a dance-floor?'

'Never. Have you?'

'Never. I like new experiences.'

Some of his frustration escaping in spite of himself, Teal said, 'Do you? I'm not so sure. I'm a new experience for you, aren't I—a man who's not falling all over you on the first date? And frankly I think it's irritating the hell out of you.'

She felt as though he had slapped her. Stepping back, her smile congealed on her face like a clown's mask, Julie said in a thin voice, 'Enough's enough. I want to go home.'

'Don't forget the eyes in the back of Nick's head,' he taunted, and led her off the dance-floor.

Somehow Julie got through saying goodbye to Bruce and Marylee without telling them precisely what she thought of their best friend; she stalked out to Teal's car and sat in a frigid silence all the way home. He pulled up by the curb and said, 'I'll walk you to the door.'

Not deigning to argue, she preceded him up the path between the velvet-petalled petunias. Putting her key in the door, she said, 'We have just had our first and our last date. Goodnight, Teal.'

To her fury he looked not the slightest bit put out. 'I rather doubt that,' he said. 'Goodnight.'

She opened the door, composing her features for the sitter, and closed it behind her. Ten minutes late, the sitter having departed in a taxi, Julie was stripping off her make-up in front of the bathroom mirror.

The trouble was, she thought, scouring her cheeks with cleansing cream, there had been an element of truth in what Teal had said. Despite his warning her to the contrary, she had seen him as a challenge. She had wanted to penetrate his armour and find the real man within.

Tonight she had found out that there was no real man. Just a consummate actor who had manipulated her feelings from beginning to end. A lawyer on duty twenty-four hours a day and always one step ahead of her, who lusted after her but cared not one whit for her feelings.

She had lived with an actor for nearly nine years; she didn't need another one; and she thoroughly disliked lawyers. Whereas if it was lust she wanted she need go no further than Nick.

As far as she was concerned, any agreements between her and Teal were dead in the water.

*   *   *

A week passed, during which Teal did not get in touch with Julie. She told herself she was glad he'd taken the hint, and jumped every time the telephone rang.

It wasn't ringing as much as it had. Apparently the symphony benefit had accomplished something.

She worked four day shifts, slept badly most nights and devoted her free time to the garden and her son. The trouble was that Scott came along with Danny. And Scott, with his dark hair and gray eyes, reminded her acutely of his father.

On a Tuesday evening, as restless as Einstein watching a flock of birds, she decided to take Danny to the Dairy Queen for an ice-cream. He'd enjoy the outing and it would get her out of range of the telephone.

Danny was playing with Scott in the tree house in Teal's back garden. So she had two choices. She could phone Teal and ask him to send Danny home. Or she could walk over there and get Danny herself. The latter seemed a much preferable course of action because she wouldn't have to speak to Teal at all.

She put on a long skirt made of turquoise crinkled cotton and a matching top with a round neckline and cap sleeves, so that she looked very different from the dancer in the spangled dress, and set off down the street.

It was a beautiful summer evening. Lawn sprinklers hissed in the front gardens, the drops of water catching the sun's rays; the bright colors of the flowers lightened her step. She needed to cultivate a sense of perspective, she told herself, admiring a particularly elegant Turkish lily in the garden next to Teal's. The agreement, brief though it had been, had done its work and she could live very well without a man. Particularly one as complicated and inaccessible as Teal.

Jauntily she walked up his driveway. The black BMW was parked under the shade of a giant old oak tree. She passed it, pushed her way through a tangle of shrubbery into the back garden and called Danny's name.

The garden was deserted except for a flock of sparrows scratching in the undergrowth. The boys must be inside.

She almost turned around to go home. But Teal had given her orchids because of her courage, and she couldn't avoid him forever. Why not see him now and get it over with?

Feeling as though she was on her way to the dentist with a mouth full of cavities, she marched up the steps and knocked on the back door, which was ajar. From inside she heard Teal yell, 'Would you get that, Scott?' and her heart gave an uncomfortable lurch. Please answer the door, Scott, she thought, rubbing her palms down the sides of her skirt.

However, neither Scott nor Danny came running through the kitchen to find out who was there. Chewing on her lip, Julie knocked again, and was rewarded by the slap of bare feet taking the stairs two at a time. They were a man's footsteps, not a boy's. Adjusting her face muscles into a smile that was a nicely judged mixture of politeness and disdain, Julie waited.

Teal swung the door open. 'Julie!' he exclaimed, and his heart jolted in his chest as if he'd touched a live wire.

He was wearing the navy sweatpants she remembered so well, and was bare-chested. Smothering any pretensions the tiger might have to rearing its head, trying to ignore that Teal looked exhausted, Julie quoted nastily, '"If my son's to spend time in your house, I'd much prefer you to keep the doors locked." Would you get him for me, please?'

'You're a woman alone in the house—there's a difference.'

She bit back a number of replies ranging from the merely catty to the obscene, and repeated, 'I'd like to speak to Danny.'

'Come in—he must be up in the attic; I'll get him.'

'Perhaps you could just send him home for me.'

'Oh, come in, Julie,' Teal said impatiently. 'I don't bite.'

As meekly as a feudal maiden, she did as she was told. The kitchen was a mess. Teal said defensively, 'Mrs Inkpen couldn't come yesterday, and I've been working night and day on a case.'

'The perfect lawyer,' she said ironically.

'You really don't like lawyers, do you?'

Realizing she was itching for a fight, she said concisely, 'I don't. I paid a lawyer a lot of money to arrange the financial side of the divorce, Robert moved back to New York and isn't paying support, and in order to do anything I'll have to get two more lawyers, one here and one there—all at my expense, you understand.'

'We're not all like that.'

She raised her brows in delicate disbelief. 'No?'

'No!' His hands gripped the edge of the kitchen table, which was littered with dirty dishes, he leaned forward and said with passionate intensity, 'This case I'm working on . . . I'm representing a fourteen-year-old boy who shot and wounded his father on the back steps of his house. In cold blood, supposedly.

'I don't think it was in cold blood; I think the kid— and his mother—have been abused since he was born and he finally got big enough to turn on the man who did it. So it's up to me to get the boy's story out of him, and to tell that story in court and make sure he gets a fair deal, including the best counseling on family violence that's available, so we can break the pattern and he won't end up abusing his own children.

'Sure, the system goes wrong, and sure, rehabilitation can be the worst joke there is—but it's all we've got and for the kid's sake I'll raise heaven and earth and work night and day if I have to.'

Julie said dazedly, 'So you do have feelings.'

'Oh, go to hell.'

'You keep them all for your work, that's all.'

Wishing he hadn't revealed a part of himself he preferred to keep private, Teal rapped, 'I happen to have feelings for my son, too—in case you hadn't noticed.'

'You're a very good father,' Julie said and gave him her most generous smile. 'The only person you're not looking after is yourself.' She glanced around her. 'I'll help you clean up the dishes if you like.'

'You came here for Danny.'

She clasped her cold fingers behind her back and said lightly, 'To take him to the Dairy Queen. We could all go after the dishes are done.'

'Julie, I warned you not to see me as a challenge.'

'It's a warning I'm choosing to ignore.'

'You'll get hurt if you do. Because I won't change.'

'I don't believe that.'

'Then you're being very foolish,' he said shortly.

They were facing each other like adversaries across the width of the table. 'You say you admire my honesty, yet you don't like it when I'm honest,' Julie cried with the courage of desperation. 'I've discovered something about you the last few minutes—that you're a man of passion and deep feelings . . . and I'm not talking about sex. You can't hide from me any more, not like you did at the dance last week. I've found you out.'

He pounded his fist on the table with a force that made the glasses rattle. 'I'm not going to get involved with you—do you hear me?' he exploded, and wondered who he was trying to convince, her or himself.

Julie's impulse was to run. She stood her ground and said, 'You asked me once if I loved my husband and I gave you a truthful answer to what was a hard question. Now I'm going to ask you a hard question. Did you love your wife, Teal? Did you love Elizabeth?'

Tension ripped along his nerves. 'I don't want to talk about Elizabeth. Not to you or to anyone else.'

In pure anticlimax Danny called down the stairs, 'Is that you, Mum? Come on up and see our fort in the attic.'

Julie let out her pent-up breath, rubbing her hands down the side of her skirt. 'I'll be back in a minute,' she said. Then she walked past Teal and into the hallway.

The house had the gracious proportions of an earlier generation, the banisters polished oak, the high ceilings decorated with ornate plaster moldings. But again she noticed the absence of paintings or plants that might have given life and form to the empty corners.

She climbed the stairs, smiling up at Danny, who was hanging over the railings. He said, 'Wait there a minute; I've got to tell Scott you're coming.'

He disappeared. She was standing on the second floor, and right in front of her was the open door to Teal's bedroom. A sweater she recognized was flung over one corner of the big bed.

Drawn by a curiosity she could not have denied, Julie stepped closer and looked inside. Tall windows over-looked the back garden, the leaves of the trees making a verdant network through the sheer curtains. The walls were white, the expensive bedspread and the plush carpet a light blue, while the furniture was made of pale pine.

She was suddenly cold, chilled to the bone, not even the surface untidiness of the room giving her comfort. Because this was the room Teal had shared with

Elizabeth? Was that what was wrong—she was jealous of a dead woman? Or was it something deeper than that?

Her eyes wandered around the room. There were photographs of Scott on the dresser, and a formal portrait of a young woman with her hair pulled back severely from a face that had an austere beauty. Then, her breath catching in her throat, Julie noticed something else. In front of the portrait, in a tiny crystal vase, was the pink rosebud she had given Teal last week. It was drooping now, the petals rusted round the edges. But he had taken the trouble to put it in water, and he had kept it in his bedroom.

Why? Why on earth had he done that?

CHAPTER SEVEN

'WHERE are you, Mum?'

Guiltily Julie backed out of Teal's bedroom. After following Danny up a narrow flight of stairs, she found herself in a roomy attic that would have been any child's delight. She crawled into the fort on her hands and knees, tested out the camp bed and consumed emergency rations consisting of dry cookies and lurid pink fruit punch. As she extricated herself from the door flaps, she said, 'I want to help your dad clean up the kitchen, Scott. Then I'll take you both for an ice-cream—would you like that?'

They would. Quickly she ran downstairs and into the kitchen. Teal had put on a shirt and was rinsing off the dishes in the sink. 'I'll help,' she said, and started stashing mugs and glasses in the dishwasher.

He was scrubbing at a plate with fierce energy. She gathered up the knives and said in a conversational tone of voice, 'You kept my rose.'

Teal jammed a plate in the rack and said in utter fury, 'Do you always go snooping in other people's bedrooms?'

'I wanted to see if it was as colorless as the rest of the house.'

'I had nothing to do with decorating this place— Elizabeth chose the color schemes when we moved in eight years ago.'

'Oh,' said Julie. 'You haven't changed a thing since she died?'

'No,' he said curtly.

Because he was overwhelmed with grief and couldn't bear to undo his wife's handiwork—was that the reason? If only she knew the answer to that question, she might understand what made Teal the way he was.

'Why did you keep the rose?' she asked in a small voice.

Teal stared at the water gurgling down the drain. He could follow the letter of the agreement and fob her off with an easy answer; or he could opt for the truth.

He said, 'Giving me that rose was important to you— it didn't seem right just to turf it.'

Almost inaudibly she answered, 'Thanks, Teal—that was sweet of you.'

He looked over at her. She was placing spoons in tidy rows in the cutlery basket and looked deep in thought. Forks followed the spoons into the basket, then she picked up a cloth to wipe the table.

'You know what?' she said suddenly. 'I think we need to renegotiate the agreement. I'm getting tired of fighting all the time.'

Speaking the truth could get to be a habit, Teal thought wryly. 'The only way we won't fight is if we never see each other.'

'What a pessimist you are.' Handing him the last dirty plate, Julie said, 'It's very simple. I want sex and you don't. I did my best to shake you up with the dress I wore to the dance, but that backfired—you accused me of sleeping with Nick and you didn't take me to bed to prove your manhood. You were right—it's the wrong plot. You're the most strong-willed man I've ever met and I can see it's useless for me to try and change your mind.'

She put a couple of clean knives away in the drawer and added, puzzled, 'Why do you keep the bicycle-repair kit in with the cutlery?'

'That's Mrs Inkpen. Her method of tidying up is to sweep everything off the counters into the nearest drawer. Don't change the subject.'

Julie laughed. 'I bet I'd like Mrs Inkpen—her filing system is the very antithesis of a lawyer's. Now, where was I?'

'You were talking about sex. You want it and I don't. Are you referring to sex with me, by the way?'

'Absolutely,' she said, wiping the counter with a flourish. 'I've never gone to bed with anyone except Robert...my upbringing left me with certain principles, one of which was called fidelity. But to get back to the agreement. Celibacy is an "in" word in all the magazines these days, and I'm sure it won't hurt me. So I suggest we change tack. No more kisses. No more close dancing. Let's just have some fun.'

'Fun?' Teal repeated quizzically.

'Mmm...like taking the boys to the Dairy Queen. Going to the beach with them, or for bicycle rides. That sort of thing.'

'You figure we wouldn't scrap that way?'

She wrinkled her nose at him. 'Well, it's worth a try, don't you think? considering we've got more than two months before the agreement runs out.'

Deliberately testing her, Teal let his gaze linger on her face and said huskily, 'That outfit you're wearing—it makes your eyes look as blue as the sea.'

'That's just the sort of thing you shouldn't do,' she cried. 'When you look at me like that—as if I'm the only woman in the world—all I want to do is make wild, passionate love with you. I wore this skirt because I was trying to cover as much of my anatomy as I could.'

'Julie, you could wear a canvas tent and still cause a traffic jam.'

'You've got to stop saying things like that,' she ordered. 'The new agreement won't allow for them. No sex. Not even a breath of it.'

'We'd be like brother and sister?' he remarked innocently.

Not all Julie's powers of imagination could picture Teal as her brother. 'That's how we'd behave,' she said firmly, and waved a slotted spoon at him. 'It's summer, Teal, and the boys are off school! Let's get out and enjoy ourselves, that's all I'm saying. After all, if we go to the Dairy Queen and the beach, people are bound to see us together—which is the whole point, isn't it?'

Quickly she stopped speaking as Danny and Scott rushed into the kitchen. Danny said, 'Are we going to get ice-cream, Mum?'

'Are you coming with us, Dad?' Scott cried.

Knowing how much was resting on his answer, Teal said, 'Sure, I'm coming . . . give us five minutes to finish the dishes.'

With loud whoops the boys took off into the garden. Teal attacked the pile of saucepans while Julie, for once, said nothing. When the last pot had been put away, Teal ran upstairs to change into a pair of jeans and Julie went outside.

Dusk was falling, the garden full of mysterious shadows. She was going to the Dairy Queen with Teal and Scott and Danny, she thought, and felt happiness well up in her heart.

Teal joined her on the step. 'Ready?'

'Could we stop off at my place so I can get my purse?'

'I'll treat you.'

'I'd rather pay for myself, Teal.'

'No scrapping, remember?' he said with a lazy grin.

'That doesn't mean you're always going to get your own way,' she announced. 'This isn't about me losing my independence.'

'Tonight it is,' he replied, putting his hands on her shoulders to turn her around and steer her in the direction of the car.

'No sex', she had said blithely a few minutes ago. What a joke, she now thought. When I'm within a mile of this man I can't keep my mind out of the bedroom. I'm the one who's going to have to learn about control.

The Dairy Queen was crowded. They bought their ice-cream and drove home, sitting at the picnic table under the maple tree. Moths danced around the porch light as the boys delved into their sundaes enthusiastically, Danny waving his spoon as he told his mother about the new additions to the tree house.

'Oops!' he said suddenly. 'I got chocolate on your sweater, Mum.'

Julie looked down. 'Darn...it's brand-new. I'll put some cold water on it,' she said, pushing herself up from the table.

'I'll get a clean cloth for you,' Teal said, following her into the kitchen and opening one of the drawers. He turned on the cold tap, wetting the cloth, and said, 'Hold still.'

The chocolate had landed just above her left breast. He held the soft knit fabric away from her body and scrubbed at it, his dark hair only inches from her face. No sex, Julie thought frantically, and all the while her eyes, greedy for him, were noting the arch of his brow, the strong jut of his cheekbone under the tanned skin, the slight shadow of his beard along his jawline. Then he looked up. His hands stilled. 'You're not remotely like a sister to me,' he said.

She could feel his breath on her cheek. 'The boys will be wondering what we're up to,' she answered weakly.

He let go of her sweater. Beneath it her nipples had hardened; dry-mouthed, he said, 'I think I got most of the chocolate out.'

The stain was the last thing on her mind. Heat scorching her cheeks, Julie stepped back and said over-loudly, 'Celibacy is an entirely viable option and will no doubt build strength of character.'

In a strained voice Teal said, 'You've met lots of men the last few months...why me?'

She remembered the chill that had struck her bones in his bedroom and let the words spill out. 'There's a place I find myself in sometimes—after all, who doesn't?—a place of loneliness where I know that, no matter who I'm with, I'm all alone. But you, I think, live in that place. Nearly all the time.'

'So you feel sorry for me,' he said harshly.

'Oh, no, it's not that simple. It's as though I can't help myself, Teal, as though something about you calls to me instinctually.' She hugged her breasts, feeling the wet fabric cling to her skin. 'Let's drop the subject, okay? You've made it abundantly clear you don't want to make love with me, and talking about it just gets me all riled up.'

'I'm beginning to realize that being chased by Janine and Cindy Thurston and Carole was an exceedingly simple form of existence compared with being in the same room with you,' Teal responded tersely. 'We'd better go back out—the ice-cream will have melted.'

Like me, Julie thought, and in a swirl of skirts ran outside. So far her renegotiated agreement didn't seem to be meeting with much success. It was probably a measure of the naïveté Robert had often accused her of that she had suggested it in the first place.

Glumly she took a mouthful of chocolate and runny ice-cream, and half an hour later was back in her own house with Danny.

On Thursday evening at eight o'clock Teal drove into Julie's driveway on his bicycle, Scott and Danny close behind him. Julie had worked from seven until seven; he had it in his mind to take her for a drink downtown and then suggest to her that they all go to the beach on Saturday. For fun. As he leaned his bicycle against the fence, the boys took off into the garden to dig for worms; Teal had promised to take them both fishing the next day. He knocked on the back door and heard Julie call in a distracted voice, 'Come in.'

He walked into the kitchen, which looked rather worse than his had a couple of days ago. Then Julie came in from the living-room. Her hair was damp from the shower, she was wearing faded, very tight-fitting jeans and a sloppy sweatshirt, and she looked as distracted as she had sounded.

'Teal,' she said. 'How are you? I——'

Then an older woman, elegantly clad in a crisp linen suit and immaculate white pumps, tapped her way into the room on Julie's heels. Julie shot a hunted look round the kitchen and said, 'This is Teal Carruthers, Mrs LeMarchant; he's a friend of mine. Teal, I'd like you to meet my landlady, Mrs LeMarchant . . . she's here for a visit.'

'How do you do, Mr Carruthers?' Ethelda LeMarchant said, managing in one glance to make Teal aware that his hair needed combing and his shirt was missing a button.

He shook hands, hoping there wasn't any bicycle grease on his fingers, exchanged some small talk with her and heard her say, 'Well, I must be going . . .'

The back door burst open and the boys raced in.
Danny was dangling a plump, shiny worm in one hand,
scattering mud on the floor with the other. 'Look at this
one, Mum,' he cried. 'It's the biggest worm I ever saw.
Can I keep it in my bedroom?'

'Say hello to Mrs LeMarchant, Danny,' Julie said
faintly. 'And this is Scott Carruthers, Teal's son.'

Neither boy could have been called clean. Mrs
LeMarchant acknowledged them with chilly politeness,
said, 'Perhaps we can get together for tea sometime this
week, Mrs Ferris, to talk over the lease . . . a pleasure to
have met you, Mr Carruthers,' and headed for the back
door. As the screen shut behind her and her steps clicked
down the driveway, Julie sat down on the nearest stool,
buried her face in her hands and burst into tears.

Teal took an instinctive step toward her. But Danny
beat him to it. The little boy dropped the worm on the
counter and made a bee line for his mother, flinging his
arms around her and burrowing into her body. 'It's okay,
Mum—you don't have to be scared of worms; they're
not like rats.'

Julie wrapped her arms around him and sobbed
harder. 'It's n-nothing to do with the worms, Danny.'

Scott looked aghast at the sight of a grown-up
weeping; his mother would never have cried in front of
him, Teal was certain. He said calmly, 'Tell you what,
boys—why don't you turn on the television in the living-
room? There's a nature show on Channel 19. I'll make
Julie some tea and find out what's upsetting her.'

Julie looked up, her face blotchy with tears, and
dropped a kiss on her son's blond curls. 'That's a g-
good idea,' she snuffled. 'I'll be all right in a few minutes,
Danny. Truly it was nothing to do with you.'

Danny butted his head against her sleeve and said with a fierce protectiveness that brought a lump to Teal's throat, 'I love you, Mum.'

She swiped at her nose with the back of her hand, giving him a singularly sweet smile. 'I love you, too. I know I'll feel better if I talk to Teal for a while, so off you go. But put the worm in the jar with the rest of them, or it'll dry out.'

After Teal had filled the kettle, he rinsed out a couple of mugs in the sink and put teabags in the pot. Then he pulled Julie to her feet, deliberately drawing her against the length of his body. 'Tell me what's the matter.'

For once she didn't feel like arguing. Instead she put her arms around his waist and sagged against him with a deep sigh. 'You feel good. Sort of solid. Like that old maple tree in your back garden by the picnic table.'

Her damp hair, which was tickling his nose, smelled fragrantly of shampoo. 'No sex', she'd said. But her weight, warm and entrancingly soft, was pressed into his body, and he was almost sure she wasn't wearing a bra. He said, feeling not at all like a chunk of wood, 'Tell me why you were crying.'

'I had a horrible day at work,' she mumbled. 'Everything went wrong that could go wrong. One of the interns botched a prescription and tried to blame me, I dropped a bag of lipids and it burst all over my brand-new shoes, a patient we thought had stabilized had to go back to ICU—and that was only the morning. This afternoon I had to do rounds with Dr Reid, and you know how I feel about her. Then an hour before my shift ended they brought up three new patients and the man in 326 had a heart attack.'

As she gave a reminiscent shudder Teal comfortingly, 'One of those days when you should stayed in bed.'

'You said it. After I got home I was just getting out of the shower when my landlady dropped in. I didn't think she was arriving until the weekend, and I'd planned to clean the house from end to end. But it's a disaster area right now. Einstein's shedding, Danny's toys and my sewing are spread all over the living-room carpet—and you can see the kitchen; your Mrs Inkpen would have a field day. The worm on the counter was the finishing touch.'

'You're paying rent, Julie; you've got a right to be untidy. And it's not very ethical of her to drop in unannounced.'

'Oh—I hadn't thought of it that way.' She looked up, her pulse leaping at the concern in his face. 'I'm paying eight hundred dollars a month. That's over a dollar an hour—you're right, I should be able to be messy. Although she did ask me to keep the house in apple-pie order.'

'An apple pie isn't a particularly tidy dish,' Teal commented.

'Pastry flaking all over the place.'

'Juice bubbling over the oven.'

Julie smiled, reluctantly edging free of his embrace. 'I feel better—thanks for the use of the shoulder.'

'Any time,' Teal said, and discovered with a twinge of pure panic that he meant it. 'We came to see if Danny could go fishing tomorrow morning,' he added hurriedly. 'And I thought the four of us might go to the beach on Saturday.'

'You're taking tomorrow off?' she asked in surprise.

He grinned. 'I won my case.'

'The one with the boy? Oh, Teal, I'm so happy for you!'

This time Julie threw her arms around him rather than sagging against him; but there was the same delicious sense of holding all the softness, energy and warmth of a woman who was fully alive. She was laughing up at him, a laughter all the more precious for her recent tears. Julie knew what emotions were all about, he thought dazedly. She lived them.

Not like Elizabeth.

The renegotiated agreement was about fun, not sex. The devil with the agreement, Teal thought, pulling her hard to his chest as, with a distinct lack of anything that could be called technique, he kissed her open mouth. A tiny shock ran through her. The long curves of her body, the yielding sweetness of her lips excited him beyond measure. He forgot that their two sons were in the next room and that he'd promised to keep his distance, forgot that he'd sworn, two years ago, never to lose control of his sexuality again. He forgot everything but his own primitive hunger for the woman in his arms.

Her tongue danced with his. His hand found the swell of her breast through the loose folds of her sweater and he discovered that he was right—she wasn't wearing a bra. With a fierce impatience he fumbled for the hem of the sweater, and then felt, under his palm, the smooth warmth of her belly.

She strained closer to him, her fingers tangled in his hair. 'Julie...' he said exultantly and blindly reached for the firm rise of her breast under her sweater. As she shivered with pleasure, making a tiny sound in her throat, he found himself looking straight into her eyes, smoke-blue eyes that were ablaze with passion.

With his free hand he smoothed back her hair, saying in a choked voice, 'You want me, Julie...you really want me,' and even as he spoke wondered how he had found the words through the turmoil of emotion in his

She took his palm and pressed it to her side, he could feel the heavy pounding of her heart. '

I want you,' she whispered. 'What is it, Teal? Why do you even need to say that?'

He couldn't begin to tell her; the phrases wouldn't formulate themselves, and the words caught in his throat. Helplessly he buried his face in the shining weight of her hair, feeling its dampness cool against his cheek. She said so softly that he had to strain to hear her, 'You can tell me, Teal—you can trust me.'

'If I trusted anyone, it would be you,' he muttered.

'When you're ready, you will tell me.'

Was it that simple? Surely not...it couldn't be. He said in a clipped voice, knowing he was running away, 'The boys will be wondering what's going on.'

Nothing could be further from Julie's mind than the boys. 'You've done it again,' she cried. 'It's as though you drop a barrier between us—like one of those portcullises clanging to the ground in a moldy old medieval castle. I hate it when you do that!'

From behind the barrier Teal watched anger and distress battle in her face. 'I can't help it—it's the way I am,' he said in a raw voice. 'I've told you over and over not to see me as a challenge.'

So he had. With a wordless exclamation of disgust she pulled free of him. 'What's this about going fishing tomorrow?'

He outlined his plan for Danny to sleep at his house with Scott, so that they could leave early in the morning. 'I'll put the canoe on the car tonight, and take them to a lake I know where you can almost always catch some trout. I'll take good care of Danny, Julie.'

'I trust you absolutely with my son,' she said.

But not otherwise...was that the unspoken corollary? Teal didn't want to ask: he'd had enough emotion for one night. He wanted to be in the green simplicity of the woods, a fly rod in his hands. Miles from this woman who made nonsense of the way he had lived his life for the last two years.

Two years? More like eight.

Or thirty-four.

And that, less that twelve hours later, was where Teal was. He and the boys fished from the canoe for a couple of hours, then he took them to shore and made breakfast over a camp stove. The boys then wandered along the rocky shore of the lake with their spinning rods while he fished a stillwater.

The mosquitoes were bad. Maybe it was time to head home, Teal thought, and tramped through the bushes toward the cove where Scott and Danny were fishing. He was screened from them by a thicket of alders, where yellow-throated warblers were singing with piercing sweetness and frogs were croaking in ponderous bass notes; through the coarse-leaved branches he heard Scott say, 'Do you think they'll get married?' and stopped dead in his tracks.

'Who?' Danny said. 'My mum and your dad? Nope. Pass me that lure, Scott.'

'The one with the yellow tassle? Why won't they get married? I think it's a neat idea.'

With the air of one pronouncing the final word Danny said, 'I heard my mum tell my dad once that she hated being married and she'd never do it again.'

There was a silence while Scott thought this over. A mosquito whined in Teal's ear, and he knew he should push through the bushes and interrupt a conversation he was not meant to overhear. Scott said, 'They've got an agreement. Dad told me about it.'

'That's just so Mum doesn't have to date all those other guys that were bugging her.'

In a puzzled voice Scott said, 'Then why were they kissing each other in the kitchen last night?'

'You can kiss someone without getting married,' Danny said scornfully.

'Maybe they'll have a baby,' Scott offered.

Danny said, not sounding so sure of himself, 'You gotta do more than kiss to make a baby. It's like those dogs we saw in the playground.'

'Oh,' said Scott. 'That's weird.' There was another silence before he went on with the kind of dogged persistence that was part of his character, 'Still, I'd like them to get married—I really like you mum.'

'Hey!' Danny yelled. 'I've got a strike! Look, it's a real fish.'

'Keep your rod up,' Scott cried, and shouted for his father, the prospect of landing a trout diverting him from the intricacies of sex and marriage.

Teal pushed through the bushes, making rather a lot of noise, and helped Danny land a seven-inch brook trout. 'Good for you,' he said warmly, ruffling the little boy's hair, touched by his excitement. He had grown very fond of Danny, he realized, cutting a forked alder twig so that Danny could carry the fish. He certainly could no longer avoid the fact that the bonds among the four of them—he, Julie, Scott, and Danny—were becoming increasingly interwoven in a way that at some deep level made him profoundly uneasy.

Tomorrow, Julie's day off, they were all going to the beach. All four of them.

Not a wise move.

However, making a mockery of Teal's doubts, the sun was shining brightly the next morning. He was a few minutes late leaving his house; Julie was outside the bungalow waiting for him, and when she saw the black

BMW she stepped into the road, saucily raising her skirt above her knee and striking a provocative pose, her thumb raised like a hitch-hiker.

He laughed out loud, wondering if she'd ever lose the capacity to surprise him. A passing delivery truck blasted its horn, the driver shouting an appreciative comment out his window, and in a swift surge of possessiveness Teal thought, Back off, buddy, she's mine.

She wasn't his. He was a fool to think that way.

He pulled into her driveway, composed his face and climbed out of the car. Julie sauntered toward him, wearing her turquoise skirt, this time with a halter-top whose brevity raised Teal's blood-pressure several notches. He said equably, 'Good morning,' and by a considerable exercise of will did not take her in his arms.

Scott leaped out of the car, threw himself at Julie and hugged her, then ran up the back steps into the house to find Danny. Teal said flatly, 'Does he always do that?'

'That's the first time.' She grimaced. 'Do you think we should renegotiate the renegotiation?'

'I'm a pretty good lawyer and I haven't got the first idea how to go about that,' Teal said with an underlying savagery that frightened her.

'We're heading into some deep waters, Teal.'

He couldn't agree more. 'Let's head for the beach instead. I don't want to have to deal with agreements and negotiations today—it's my day off.'

She smiled, shaking off her unease and lifting her face to the heat of the sun, her hair swinging loose on her shoulders. 'You're right—it's a wonderful day!' she said.

Her beauty, so vivid and inescapable a part of her, always had the power to catch Teal off guard, and now filled him with a fierce and nameless yearning that penetrated all his defenses. Turning away from her so

that she couldn't see his face, he opened the trunk of
the car and went into the house to get their gear.

They stopped for ice-cream on the way to the beach,
and as soon as they arrived the boys stripped off their
T-shirts and ran for the ocean. Julie spread her towel on
the white sand, looking around her contentedly. 'This is
heaven,' she said. Then, trying not to feel self-conscious,
she dropped her skirt to the sand, following it with her
top.

Her bikini was also turquoise; the stretch marks on
her belly, because they made her less than perfect, because they stemmed from another man's child, caught
at Teal's heart in a complicated mingling of tenderness
and jealousy. Suddenly tired of running from his
emotions, he said huskily, 'Lie down and I'll put some
suntan lotion on your back.'

As her eyes met his, between them blazed all the complexities of unassuaged desire. She said, 'Only if you'll
let me do the same with you.'

'I don't think I've got the will-power to deny you anything right now,' Teal said.

'Then it's too bad this is a public beach,' Julie replied
stringently and lay face down on the towel, her cheek
resting on her linked hands, her eyes closed.

Keeping a weather eye on the boys, who were frolick-
ing at the water's edge, Teal began smoothing the lotion
over her shoulders. Her bra strap was in his way. He
unlinked it, his imagination running riot, and let his
palms slide over the curve of her ribcage. The suntan
lotion was an excuse; he was honest enough to admit
that—an excuse to allow his hands to explore her
nakedness for the first time, tracing the concavity of her
waist and the soft swell of her hips. His knees brushing
her legs as he knelt beside her, he smoothed the pale skin
of her inner thigh.

Julie reared her head and in a strangled voice said, 'I could, right now, pull you down on top of me and ravish you in full view of everyone else on the beach, including our two sons—I've never in my life been tempted to behave like that! It's not just me, is it, Teal? Please tell me it's not just me...that you feel the same way.'

She had twisted to face him, grabbing at her bra to cover her breasts. There was real anguish in her face.

'Why do you think I'm kneeling down?' he answered with a crooked smile that didn't reach his eyes. 'To hide the all too obvious evidence that I want you just as much as you want me.'

She glanced downward and blushed scarlet. 'Oh. That's good.'

'Good?' he repeated testily. 'Who are you kidding? It's uncomfortable, it's frustrating, and it scares the living daylights out of me.'

'That, also, is good—it's past time you admitted to some feelings!'

'I've admitted to more in the last six weeks than in my entire life,' he retorted, then could have bitten off his tongue for saying something that, indirectly, was so revealing of his marriage.

She gave him a long, thoughtful look. 'That's the truth, isn't it? You've kept everything to yourself ever since you were little.'

'This is a day off, Julie,' he said tightly. 'No agreements, no negotiations—and no psychoanalysis.'

'And no sex?' she flashed.

He suddenly laughed, a laugh that came from deep in his chest and snapped the tension between them. 'I'd be a blatant hypocrite if I agreed to that.'

A reluctant smile tugged at her mouth. 'Me, too,' she said. After fumbling with the catch on her bra, she scrambled to her feet. 'Now it's your turn,' she added.

Teal lay down, carefully, on his stomach. The first touch of lotion was cool on his skin. But Julie's hands were warm and he closed his eyes, aware through every nerve in his body of the pressure of her palms as they roamed across his shoulderblades and down his spine. No sex? he thought wildly. That was the joke of the century.

'The boys are coming,' she said. 'On the run.'

In a flurry of sand Scott skidded to a halt beside his father. 'When are you guys coming swimming?' he demanded.

'The waves are great!' Danny puffed, and mischievously laid an ice-cold hand on Teal's leg. Teal yelped. Danny and Scott screamed with laughter.

Julie said with a diplomacy that she was sure Teal would appreciate, 'I'll come with you—give your dad a minute or two to relax first.'

Right, Teal thought ironically, glancing over his shoulder as the two boys grabbed Julie's hands and ran down the beach with her. Whenever he was away from her, it seemed entirely possible to keep matters between them at the level of fun. But the minute he touched her that particular three-letter word was immediately replaced by another. A far more potent one, he thought wryly, rolling over onto his back.

He was out of control.

Out of control, and no way back.

Monday was Julie's birthday. She drove home slowly, giving herself time to bridge the gap between the hospital and home. She had brought two striploin steaks and the makings of a salad for supper; her parents would phone, and her sisters, and she would have to battle the usual homesickness that birthdays seemed to engender. She was twenty-nine, she thought, turning down her street. Next year she'd be thirty. And ten years ago she had married Robert.

None of these thoughts was particularly happy.

Cheer up, Julie, she chided herself. Twenty-nine's not old, and it'll be nice to spend a quiet evening with Danny. You're the luckiest woman in the world to have such a wonderful son.

She slowed for her driveway, then ground her gears in sheer surprise. The whole front garden was filled with pink plastic flamingoes circling a sign that said 'Happy 29th, Julie'. They were very ugly flamingoes. Smiling foolishly, she parked the car and climbed the back steps.

Einstein was sitting on the porch looking extremely bad-tempered, a big pink bow attached to his collar. He hissed at her as she opened the door.

The kitchen was full of balloons, pink and white and red. 'Happy birthday, Mum!' Danny cried. Scott jammed a paper hat on her head, yelling, 'Surprise, surprise!' and Teal stepped forward and kissed her on the mouth, putting a glass of champagne in her hand.

Her eyes awash with tears, she sat down on the nearest stool, gave them all a wobbly smile and took a big gulp of champagne. 'I didn't expect this at all,' she quavered. 'Who's responsible for the birds on the front lawn?'

'Einstein is,' Danny giggled. 'We're going out for supper downtown; Teal's taking us. And then we have to come back here for your presents.'

She looked over at the man leaning on the counter; she could still feel the warm pressure of his lips on hers. This was his doing, she knew it. 'Thank you,' she said and raised her glass in a toast to him.

He smiled back, a smile that warmed his eyes and reminded her irresistibly of the tang of the ocean and the heat of the sand and the smooth slide of a man's hands over her bare back. The gate to the castle was finally opening, she thought. But would she be invited to enter? And if invited would she have the courage to walk through the doorway?

She had hated sex with Robert.

As the bubbles of champagne exploded in her throat, she made a pledge to herself. Before she was thirty, she wanted Teal to be her lover. She had no idea how she was going to bring that about, but she wanted it more than she had even wanted anything for any of her birthdays.

She was more sure that she might succeed than she had been a couple of weeks ago; but she was still far from certain.

CHAPTER EIGHT

THE birthday party was still very much on Teal's mind a few days later as he sat in his study trying to concentrate on his latest brief. Doodling with a pen on his legal pad, he remembered how Julie had thrown herself into the celebrations with all the zest of a child. She had changed from her trim white uniform into a sundress that had made his head swim and she had thoroughly enjoyed her meal in the restaurant.

Danny had saved up his money to buy her a cake; it had been adorned with livid green and orange icing and twenty-nine red candles and had, predictably, made her both laugh and cry. Teal had arranged for two sitters, and after the boys were in bed had taken her dancing in a bar downtown.

He hadn't ravished her on the dance-floor under the strobe lights. But it had been a near thing. And he had limited himself to one kiss on her doorstep when he had taken her home, although it had been an intense, prolonged and passionate kiss that had led, also predictably, to another of the many sleepless nights he'd been having lately.

He couldn't go on like this.

But if he and Julie became lovers—a step that in itself broke him out in a cold sweat—the boys would be bound to find out. And then Scott, if not Danny, would be marching the pair of them up the aisle complete with Mendelssohn and white roses.

It was ironic, he thought, that Danny had overheard Julie's aversion to remarrying. He, Teal, had no idea whether she still felt that way. It didn't really matter. His own aversion was more than enough for the two of them—although he sincerely hoped that Scott didn't know he felt that way.

He looked down at the pad of yellow paper, where unconsciously he had been drawing a series of squares and rectangles, rigid, geometric figures with no curves, no flow or spontaneity. His pen had scored the paper deeply enough to tear it.

It would be simpler if this were just about him and Julie. But there were four people involved. If not six, he added unhappily, thinking of the handsome, debonair actor who had been married to Julie, and of Elizabeth, his own wife, who in her way had been as rigid and unspontaneous as the figures he had drawn.

The past had happened. He couldn't erase it, much as he might want to. Perhaps, he thought moodily, drawing a big bunch of balloons floating above the largest square, it had taken Julie's arrival in his life to make him realize how deeply he had been scarred by his marriage. To hear how loudly, to use her phrase, the portcullis had clanged shut.

What was he going to do?

He was not a man used to being at a loss. At work he made dozens of decisions daily, using his intelligence and an intuition gleaned from experience. And nearly always they were the right decisions. Yet now he felt paralyzed, his intelligence battling his intuition with a ferocity that immobilized him. Rational thought told him to run a mile from the woman with the tumbled hair and the smoke-blue eyes. Intuition said, Stay; she's important to you. Vital. If you run from her, you'll never get a second chance.

With deep relief he heard the thud of Scott's steps on the oak stairway; it never failed to astonish him how much noise an eight-year-old boy could make. 'I'm in the study,' he called, and shoved the legal pad in the drawer of his desk.

'Dad, could you take me to the store? I want to get some sugar. Danny and I are going to sell lemonade 'cause we need the money to get a model airplane set.'

'We'll take our bikes,' Teal said, standing up and stretching the tension from his shoulders. The exercise would do him good, and maybe when he got back he'd be able to concentrate on his job rather than his sex life.

His non-existent sex life.

And whose choice was that? No one's but his.

'I wonder what's taking Scott so long?' Danny said restlessly. He had been painstakingly squeezing lemons into a big pitcher, had emptied both ice trays into the juice and now needed the sugar.

'Maybe his dad couldn't take him right away,' Julie said soothingly. She had just gotten home from work. She'd had a relatively peaceful shift and had been able to catch up on some paperwork, and tonight she planned to go to bed early in the hopes of catching up on her sleep. The trouble was, she didn't want to sleep alone any more. She wanted Teal beside her in the bed.

As she got a mug out of the cupboard and plugged in the kettle, Danny's voice broke into her train of thought. 'Can I take my bike and see if Scott's home yet?'

'Sure. Stay on the sidewalk, though.'

She made her favorite Earl Grey tea. Taking the mug out on the back porch, she pushed Einstein off the lawn chair, much to his displeasure, and sat down. He immediately jumped up in her lap and the tea slopped over the arm of the chair, just missing her thigh. She hastily put the mug down on the small plastic table beside her and rubbed Einstein's ears, a move that never failed to reduce him to bleary-eyed ecstasy. Julie liked Einstein. He knew what he wanted out of life and did his utmost to ensure he got it.

'I wish I could catch Teal as easily as you catch birds,' she told him, kneading his fur.

Einstein blinked complacently.

Danny peddled up the driveway and let his bike fall against the fence. 'He's not home yet,' he said disconsolately. 'His dad wouldn't have taken him for ice-cream without me, would he?'

'I'm sure he wouldn't, Danny...maybe they met someone they knew at the store. Do you want me to go over to the playground with you while you're waiting?'

Danny brightened. 'We could play catch with my new baseball glove.'

He ran inside to find it. Julie sipped her tea, stroking Einstein's fur. While she was more than happy that Danny and Scott were such close friends, at times she worried a little that they were too close. Too dependent on each other for everything.

Danny came outside brandishing his glove and she drained her mug. 'I'll have to get my sneakers,' she said. 'Two seconds.'

She went inside, found her sneakers in the very back of her closet, and was tying the laces when the telephone by her bed rang. She picked up the receiver and said, 'Hello?'

There was a pause, then a small voice said, 'Julie?'

'Yes, it's Julie...is that you, Scott? Speak up, dear, I can hardly hear you.'

'Julie, my dad...' His voice trailed away altogether.

Gripping the receiver, filled with a sudden cold terror, Julie said sharply, 'Scott, where are you? What's wrong?'

Voices spoke in the background. Then a woman said, 'Is that Julie Ferris?'

In an agony of impatience Julie said, 'Yes . . . please tell me what's wrong.'

'It's Rita Glassco, from Emergency. Scott's father was hit by a car; he's being looked at now. Possible head and chest injuries, not sure what else. Scott wanted to phone you.'

Julie liked Rita, who was also a single parent. 'I'll be there as soon as I can,' she said rapidly. 'Rita, would you let me speak to Scott again, please?' After a pause she heard the sound of Scott's breathing. 'Scott,' she said as forcibly as she could, 'Danny and I will come right away—we'll be there in ten minutes. And Scott, your dad will be all right, do you hear me?'

'Yeah,' he said, sounding anything but convinced.

Julie grabbed her purse, ran for the back door and quickly explained to Danny what had happened. 'Hop in the car while I lock up.'

She drove the shortest route to the hospital, agonizing over every red light, blasting her horn at a couple of tourists who couldn't decide which lane to take and ended up blocking both. But finally she pulled up in the nurses' parking lot. Taking Danny's hand firmly in hers, she ran to the emergency department.

It was in its usual state of controlled chaos. Rita was talking on the phone at the main desk, and when she saw Julie gestured to the second waiting-room. Julie hurried down the hall and walked into the room. Several people were sitting in the chairs lined up against the wall; but she had eyes only for Scott. He was hunched over, staring at the scuffed toes of his Adidas sneakers with a dull misery that frightened her out of her wits. He looked like a child who had totally lost hope.

Teal wasn't dead . . . he couldn't be.

'Scott, we're here,' she said.

He looked up and in one convulsive movement flung himself at her. She staggered under his weight, knelt on the floor and wrapped her arms around him, holding him hard; he was trembling all over. Gathering Danny into her embrace as well, she asked urgently, 'Have you seen your dad yet, Scott?' He shook his head. 'Have they said what's wrong with him?' His dark hair, so like Teal's, rubbed against her cheek in denial.

'I know the nurse at the desk—let's go find out what's happening,' she said.

But he clutched her all the harder. It didn't take much sensitivity to realize that he was terrified of what he might hear; as, indeed, was she. 'We'll all go together,' she said. 'Come on, love.'

He glued himself to her side and allowed himself to be steered to the main desk; Rita put her hand over the receiver of the telephone and said hastily, 'They were taking Mr Carruthers up to X-Ray, and they'll bring him back to Room 9... Sorry, sir, you were saying?'

Room 9 was empty. Julie stood irresolutely in the hall. She could go up to the X-ray department or she could wait here. Then her dilemma was solved for her. A stretcher was wheeled round the corner. The man on it was Teal.

His eyes were closed and his face drained of color. The skin had been scraped from one cheek and all down his arm. His chest was bare. Then, in sheer terror, she saw that one of the doctors accompanying the stretcher was Nick.

Nick was a neurosurgeon. Neurosurgeons were only called in for serious injuries.

I love Teal, she thought with the clarity of true despair. I love him...he can't die.

Nick looked up, saw her standing there and came toward her, giving her the intimate smile he bestowed on all women who were over sixteen and under sixty. 'Julie, what a nice surprise . . . what are you doing here?'

Torn by a paralyzing fear, fury that Nick could be so callous, and the sheer wonder of her discovery, she faltered. 'Teal . . . what's wrong with him?'

'What are you talking about?'

'For God's sake, Nick—this is Teal on the stretcher,' she cried. 'Tell me what's wrong with him—I have to know!'

'Oh, he's not my patient,' Nick said casually.

'He's *not*?'

Nick grabbed Julie's sleeve. 'You look like you're going to faint...here, sit down.' He turned to the intern. 'What's the problem with Carruthers?'

'Concussion, three broken ribs, contusions and bruising,' the intern replied. 'He'll be here for a day or so.'

'Nothing serious,' Nick remarked. 'You surprise me, Julie; that evening at the symphony benefit I got the impression you and Teal were antagonists more than lovers.'

Ignoring Nick, she grasped the intern's white sleeve and said over-loudly, 'That's the truth? You're not hiding anything?'

'You can see the chart,' Nick interposed in an annoyed voice.

Aware that she was behaving very unprofessionally, Julie stooped down by Scott and said in the same loud voice, 'He's all right, Scott. He'll be in hospital for a couple of days and then he'll be home.'

But Scott was staring at his father's motionless form on the stretcher and gave no evidence of having heard her. 'He's not dead,' she said violently. Scott gave her a blank look and said nothing. Desperate to get through to him, Julie took the boy's hand in hers and laid it on Teal's bare chest. 'See,' she said, 'he's breathing; can you feel it?'

Teal's torso was rising and falling slowly and steadily. Scott's lashes flickered. He said in a thin voice, 'He's not dead?'

'He's breathing, sweetheart,' she repeated forcefully. 'He's going to be all right.'

In the same emotionless voice Scott said, 'I thought he was dead. Like my mum.'

Julie's face contorted with compassion. Having no idea what to say, she put her arms around Scott and held him as tightly as she could, feeling tears of relief and pity stream down her cheeks, and wishing Scott would cry as well.

Nick said officiously, 'You'll have to move, Julie; you're blocking the corridor.'

The attendant was wheeling the stretcher down the hall, the intern briskly walking alongside it. Half carrying Scott, Danny trailing along behind her, Julie followed the little cavalcade into the treatment-room. The intern said, 'The orthopaedic resident will be along to tape him up. Then we'll get him a room upstairs. Shouldn't be too long.'

'Do you know what happened?' Julie asked.

'Car went through a stop sign and ran into his bicycle.' The intern shrugged. 'He was lucky—could have been a lot worse.'

He could have been killed, Julie thought, and felt the same fierce upwelling of terror and love in her breast. If she had ever pictured falling in love again, she had envisioned a moonlit night and sweetly scented summer roses and herself in a filmy dress with flowers in her hair. Not blue jeans and a bare hospital room and two frightened little boys as her companions.

The intern left the room. Julie sat down on the only chair, pulled Scott on to her lap and held Danny in the circle of her other arm. 'Broken ribs are painful, but not serious, Scott,' she said. 'The doctors'll probably keep your dad in hospital a couple of days because they like to watch a concussion. Truly he'll be all right.'

Scott's eyes were glued to the motionless figure on the stretcher, and she wasn't at all sure that he had heard her. 'I wouldn't lie to you, Scott!'

Without turning his head, he said with stony politeness, 'The policeman told me my mum would be all right.'

Julie's mouth tightened. How had Elizabeth Carruthers died? Why had there been a policeman—had it been another accident? Absently stroking Scott's rigid shoulders, she knew she lacked the courage to ask him. If indeed he would answer, which she doubted.

She smiled down at Danny. 'Are you okay?'

He gave her a wordless nod. Concentrating on calming her own churned-up emotions, Julie held both boys close and waited. A nurse rushed in, checked Teal's vital signs and left, all without saying a word. Twenty minutes later the resident walked in. He had dark circles under his eyes and rumpled red hair, and had once had a long conversation with Julie in the cafeteria about white-water canoeing, a sport to which he was addicted.

'Julie—what are you doing here?' he asked.

I'm in love with the man on the stretcher . . . 'Teal Carruthers is a—a friend of mine, Steve,' she said, and rubbed her chin on Scott's head. 'This is his son.'

Steve had unclipped the X-rays and was holding them up to the light. 'Clean breaks,' he said. 'He looks in good shape, shouldn't take overly long healing . . . he'll be okay, sonny.' And he gave Scott a tired grin.

Scott stared back expressionlessly. Julie sighed. It was a good thing she had the next three days off; Scott was obviously going to need a great deal of attention.

After Steve had taped Teal's ribs with casual expertise, he said, 'Do you know if they've got him a room yet?' Julie shook her head. 'I'll check at the front desk for you; the place is a madhouse tonight. See you, Julie.' He directed another smile at Scott. 'No bicycle riding for your dad for a while,' he said, scribbled some notes on the chart, and left the room.

An hour later Teal had been transferred to a private room on the fifth floor. The move had made him restless; his eyelids were flickering and he was trying to speak, although Julie couldn't catch what he was saying. It was getting late; she should take the boys home and put them to bed. But she was reluctant to leave until Scott had at least seen his father recover consciousness.

She leaned over the bed and said softly, 'It's all right, Teal . . . we're here.'

He moved his arm, his hand searching for a hold on the smooth white coverlet. As pain convulsed his features, his eyes flew open, looking straight at her. His irises opaque with bewilderment, he whispered, 'Julie?'

But before she could reply his confusion was ripped aside by an overriding terror. 'Scott—where's Scott?' he burst out, trying to push himself up from the bed. But the effort was too much for him. With an animal sound of pure agony he collapsed back on the pillow.

Feeling as inept as a student on her first night on the wards, Julie put her palm on his chest and said clearly, 'Scott's right here—he wasn't hurt at all. Do you hear me, Teal? Scott's here by the bed.'

Teal's chest was heaving as he fought the pain down, his struggle so apparent and so intense that Julie felt tears crowd her eyes. She blinked them back; this was no time for her to cry. Then he opened his eyes again. She hitched Scott halfway up the metal railings on the bed and watched Teal's vision focus on his son, a frown of fierce concentration furrowing his brow.

'Scott,' he said hoarsely. 'I was so afraid you'd been hit...'

Scott shook his head. Although Julie could feel that the boy was trembling again, his face gave nothing away. Teal's eyes had flooded with tears of weakness; Scott's were dry. She said with a calmness she was far from feeling, 'I'll take him to my place until you're home... I don't have to work so I can look after him through the day as well.'

'Thanks,' Teal muttered. With an obvious effort of will he looked straight at his son. 'I love you, Scott,' he said.

The effort had exhausted him; his eyes closed. Julie, who would have given a great deal to have Teal say those words to her, said quietly, 'Scott, if you're ready to leave, I think we should go. Your dad needs all the rest he can get and he knows you're all right now. Why don't we go home and I'll make you both some hot chocolate before you go to bed?'

Scott wriggled free, sliding to the floor. 'Okay,' he said in a dull voice.

'We can phone first thing in the morning to see how he is,' she added, wishing she knew what was going on in his head.

'You can sleep in my bed if you want,' Danny offered. Scott smiled minimally, slipping his hand into Julie's, and walked out of the room without a backward look. Julie asked the floor nurse to let them know if there was any change in Teal's condition, then took the boys home. She made up the other bunk bed in Danny's room, found Scott a pair of Danny's pajamas, added extra marshmallows to the hot chocolate and read several chapters from one of the more soothing of her son's eclectic collection of books.

Danny fell asleep. She tucked Scott in, kissing him goodnight. 'I'm in the next room if you need me and I'll leave a night light on in the hall. Sleep well, sweetheart.'

After pulling on a pair of cotton pajamas, Julie went to bed herself. She had expected to lie awake worrying about Teal, and must have fallen instantly into a deep sleep; the next thing she knew she was lying wide-eyed in the darkness wondering what had woken her. Then she heard it again: a child's thin cry of terror.

She was out of bed in a flash and into the adjoining bedroom. Danny was peacefully asleep, burrowed under the covers, Einstein curled into his knees. But Scott was thrashing under the sheets, whimpering in his sleep. Julie took him by the shoulders. 'Wake up—you're having a nightmare, Scott.'

His head jerked up and he grabbed her, clinging to her as though he would never let go, his thin little body shaking violently. It took Julie a minute to realize that he was crying; with a pang of acute pity she heard the words that he was mumbling into her shoulder over and over again, 'I want my mum, I want my mum...'

Instinctively she gathered him into her arms and lay down beside him, pulling the blankets round him. He cried for a long time before, between one breath and the next, he fell asleep. Julie lay still in the darkness. Somehow she had to find out what had happened to Scott's mother.

Nor did she change her mind in the morning. The boys hadn't been up for half an hour before Scott picked a fight with Danny and was openly rude to her when she intervened, behavior so unlike him that she was nonplussed. Yet when they approached the main door of the hospital that afternoon, Scott was clutching her hand so tightly he was hurting her.

Teal was propped up in bed when she led the boys into his room. Conquering the urge to throw herself at him as Scott had thrown himself at her, she said with commendable lightness, 'Your face looks like you collided with a dump truck, not a car. How are you feeling?'

'Like I collided with a dump truck,' he said with a careful smile. 'Whatever else you do, don't make me laugh. Hi there, Danny. Scott, how are you doing, son?' He patted the bed. 'Why don't you climb up here so I can give you a hug?'

Julie took Danny to the cafeteria for an ice-cream, and when she went back upstairs asked both boys to wait in the recreation-room down the hall because she needed to talk to Teal. Although he looked worn out when she went back in, she hardened her heart. Briefly she described how Scott had been behaving. 'So I need to know what happened to your wife,' she finished.

He should have realized Scott would react that way, Teal thought, his helplessness like a dead weight in his chest. Trying to gather his wits through a headache that held his forehead in a vise, he said, 'It was a senseless accident. She slipped on some ice at the edge of the road when she was walking downtown—it was in January— and fell, hitting her head against the curb. She fractured her skull and died of a haemorrhage in hospital.' Playing with the hem of the sheet, he added tersely, 'Scott was with her.'

Teal's explanation made total sense of Scott's behavior. 'So this is the second time,' Julie whispered. 'Of course he didn't believe me when I kept telling him you'd be all right. And of course he's having nightmares.'

'He is?' Julie nodded. Unable to restrain his frustration, Teal said, 'It's hardly fair to expect you to cope with all this, Julie. He's not your child—why should you be saddled with him?'

She felt as though Teal had struck her in the face. 'Surely you'd do the same for me.'

'It's still not right—especially on your days off, when you need your rest.'

'I'm not complaining, Teal,' she said, an edge to her voice. 'I needed to know what happened to Elizabeth so I'd know best how to deal with Scott's fears. That's all.'

He hitched himself higher in the bed, gasping from the pain in his ribs. 'I'm not saying I don't appreciate what you're doing—naturally I'm very grateful to you.'

Gratitude was not high on the list of emotional responses Julie wanted from Teal. But she shouldn't lose her temper with a man who had three broken ribs and a concussion. A man she loved.

'Thank you for telling me about Elizabeth,' she said stiffly. 'Do you want me to bring Scott in again this evening?'

The vise had tightened around Teal's temples, and he hated feeling so powerless. 'I could call Marylee... perhaps she could take Scott for a few days.'

'Don't you trust me?' Julie grated.

'This is about imposition. Not about trust.'

'Teal Carruthers,' she seethed, 'you're being about as obtuse as a man can be—which is pretty damned obtuse. I'm happy to look after Scott. Nor do I feel as though you're imposing him on me. Have you got that straight?'

'We'll discuss this later when I'm capable of stringing more than two sentences together,' he snarled.

She stalked to the door. 'I'll bring Scott in at seven this evening. Your problem is that you can't stand being indebted to me.'

That she was totally accurate didn't help at all. 'If I could stand upright, you wouldn't get away with walking out on me!'

She poked her head back in the door. 'Try me,' she said, and blew him a kiss. She was behaving very childishly. But there was a certain satisfaction in such behavior; which was maybe why children did it.

Scott had another nightmare at three o'clock the next morning. Again Julie woke him. As he huddled in her arms, she said gently, 'Your dad told me what happened to your mother—no wonder you were so scared when the car hit his bicycle. Why don't you tell me how it happened?'

The words spilled over one another. 'We were driving down the street and this neat black sports car was speeding at the intersection. Dad yelled at me to brake, so I did. He braked too, but the car ran into him anyway. The police said afterwards the man in the sports car had been drinking; that was why he didn't see the stop sign. Dad hit the road and there was all this blood and people standing around watching, and then the ambulance and the cruiser came and they took me to the hospital, too. That's when I phoned you.'

'You did absolutely the right thing,' she said. 'It must have been terrifying for you, Scott... Why don't you try and sleep now, and you'll feel better in the morning?'

'I was real scared,' he confessed, shoving his head under her chin.

Within moments he was asleep again, curled up against her with a trust that touched her to the heart. If she loved Teal as woman to man, she was beginning to love Scott as a mother loved a son.

What had Teal said? 'He's not your child'...

No wonder those words had hurt so much.

Her pledge to become Teal's lover now seemed rather infantile. She still wanted to make love to him; that hadn't changed. But she wanted far more than that. She wanted Teal to trust her, to let down his guard and shed his control once and for all.

She wanted a lot. The sun, the moon and the stars, she thought ruefully. The whole man and no half-measures.

Julie spent the next morning cleaning and tidying Teal's house. Then from her garden and his she purloined as many flowers as she could, putting vases of brightly colored blooms in his bedroom and the living-room and the kitchen. Scott trailed around after her, talking non-stop as though to make up for his silence the last two days. Just before lunch Teal came home.

Julie had picked him up at the hospital and driven him back to his house. He negotiated the back steps and sat down on one of the kitchen chairs to catch his breath, saying shakily, 'I feel like an old man of ninety. At this rate it'll take me fifteen minutes to make it to my bedroom.'

Scott grinned at him. 'Julie's getting lunch for us and she's cooking supper too. She made gumdrop cookies yesterday and today she vacuumed the whole house. That was nice of her, eh, Dad?'

Julie winced; she wanted no more remarks about impositions. 'It gave me an excuse not to invite my landlady over for tea,' she said.

Teal looked around, his eyes brushing over the big bouquet of shasta daisies and dahlias on the table; they couldn't by any stretch of the imagination be called colorless. 'Mrs Inkpen could learn a thing or two from you,' he said, and pushed himself up from the table. 'It's ridiculous, but I need to lie down. Will you come up with me, Scott?'

'Sure, Dad. But then I have to help Julie set the table.'

The two of them disappeared in the direction of the stairs. Looking bored, Danny sprawled himself across the nearest chair. Julie started making sandwiches. She wasn't imagining things: ever since the accident Teal had been avoiding anything that could be construed as intimacy with her. He didn't want to be beholden to her. He resented her cheering up Elizabeth's kitchen with a few flowers.

Perhaps he didn't want her here at all.

Just because she loved him, it didn't mean he loved her.

Scott took up a lunch tray, staying there while Teal ate, and trotted back down with the empty tray an hour later. 'Dad's going to have a sleep,' he reported. Julie took the boys swimming all afternoon, delaying her return as long as she could.

When she got back, Scott vanished upstairs again, Danny played listlessly in the garden, and she baked chicken legs and made a salad. This time she took the tray up herself. Teal was dozing in the big bed, the breeze wafting the curtains like sails catching the wind. Scott was curled up on one corner of the bed, reading. 'I've brought your supper, Teal,' she said.

His eyes jerked open. He had been dreaming about her; she had been driving him along a country lane in a black sports car, so fast that they were out of control. Pulling his body up in the bed, feeling sweat break out on his forehead, he wished passionately that anyone but Julie were bringing him his supper.

'Thanks,' he said briefly.

'Your supper's downstairs, Scott,' she said.

'I want to eat with my dad.'

'Let him eat up here, Julie—it's one less for you to worry about.'

Danny was missing Scott's company, but Julie was darned if she was going to say so. She prepared another tray, and after she had taken it upstairs she and Danny ate at the picnic table under the maple tree. Danny picked at his food and she had little appetite; she felt ill at ease, her senses overly alert like those of an animal waiting for a storm.

When Danny disappeared into the tree house, she went inside to clean up the kitchen. Scott brought the trays down, lingering by the sink as she rinsed off the plates. She understood why he had been staying so close to Teal ever since the accident, and was searching for the words to explain that Danny was feeling abandoned when Scott said, 'I gotta favor to ask.'

'Sure,' she said, smiling at him as she reached for the detergent.

'A big favor. A real big one.'

He was looking very serious. More cautiously she said, 'If I can.'

'I want you to marry my dad.'

The plastic bottle of detergent slipped from her fingers and thumped to the floor. She said blankly, 'I can't do that, Scott.'

'Why not?'

Because he hasn't asked me. She picked up the bottle and turned on the tap, her mind going round in circles.

'Marriage is a big step,' she hedged. 'I'm divorced and your dad's widowed, so we've both been hurt... we're not ready to get married again.'

'Danny and I have seen you kissing Dad—so you must like him.'

'I do like him. But you can't marry everyone you like.'

His jaw set in a way she recognized, Scott said, 'You mean you don't want to marry him.'

The sink was on the verge of overflowing. Julie grabbed for the tap and knew that if she were truthful she'd say, If he loved me, I'd marry him... if he'd stop being so controlled and let his feelings out, I'd marry him. Instead she said, 'I can't answer that, Scott. I know you don't understand, and I hate it when adults tell children they'll understand when they're older... but that's what I'm saying.'

Scott was rhythmically kicking the leg of one of the chairs, his face stormy—the storm she had been subconsciously waiting for, Julie realized with a sinking heart. 'It's all your fault!' he blurted. 'I like it when you're here; it's like you're my mum, and I don't see why you won't marry my dad!'

Tears were hanging on his lashes. Feeling her way, she asked, 'Have you spoken to your father about this?'

Glaring at her, he said rudely, 'Why should I? It's your fault, not his—Danny told me you wouldn't get married ever again. I wish you'd never come here!'

He ran outdoors, slamming the screen door behind him. Julie took a step after him, then halted in frustration. It was better to leave him on his own for a while; he obviously wasn't in the mood to listen to reason. So she started cleaning up the dishes, her heart like a chunk of ice in her breast; although normally nimble-fingered, she broke a glass and chipped a plate. Finally, with immense reluctance, she went upstairs.

Teal was standing by the bureau in his bedroom, trying to get his arms into a cotton shirt. As she moved to help him, he said shortly, 'I can manage.'

Her nails digging into her palms, she said, 'Teal, don't you think it would be better if I slept on the couch downstairs tonight? You're still pretty shaky on your feet.' She managed a credible smile. 'Your own personal nurse.'

It was the last thing he wanted. 'That's not necessary, Julie; I'll be fine. Anyway, you have to go to work tomorrow, don't you?'

'I could leave from here.'

Not looking at her, he said, 'Go home and get some rest—you must need it after the last couple of days.'

Everything Julie had done since his accident had been motivated by love. But she couldn't tell him that. 'You're shutting me out again,' she said.

'I'm beginning to think I *was* crazy to suggest that damned agreement. You were right—there are four of us involved here, not two, and there's a huge potential for hurting the boys.'

What about me? she wanted to scream. With careful restraint she said, 'What are you getting at?'

He straightened, knowing he didn't have the energy for any kind of a showdown. 'Nothing other than that I think you should go home tonight.'

If she lived up to her reputation for honesty and courage, she'd be telling Teal that she was in love with him—and knew she couldn't do it. Steeling herself, Julie asked, 'Is it Elizabeth who's in the way—because you still love her?'

He said violently, 'I don't want to lie to you, Julie— will you for God's sake leave it alone?'

Too proud to cry in front of him, she said quietly, 'I'm sorry... I guess I should have called Mrs Inkpen to come here today. I'll take Danny home now.'

She turned away from him and walked down the oak stairs, blind to the evening light that fell softly on the burnished wood. Picking up her handbag from the counter, she put her sweater round her shoulders because she was cold. Then, as shrill voices penetrated her distress, she realized that the boys were arguing outdoors. Through the open screen she heard Scott cry, 'It's all your mother's fault—she's the one who won't marry my dad!'

'It isn't her fault,' Danny retorted.

'It is so!'

'I bet your dad hasn't asked her. It's the man who's supposed to do the asking.'

'She'd say no even if he did,' Scott threw back. 'You told me she would. You told me she didn't like being married to your father and she didn't want to get married ever again.'

Frozen to the spot, Julie heard Danny say sulkily, 'I bet your dad could change her mind if he wanted to.' And then she heard something else: Teal's footsteps coming into the kitchen. Wishing him a thousand miles away, she stood as still as a post.

'It's not his fault,' Scott yelled. 'It's your mum who won't get married.'

'Shut up!' Danny screeched, and to her horror Julie heard a sudden thud and then bodies scuffling in the bushes. Jerked into motion, she ran outside and down the steps. Grabbing at the nearest body, she hauled Scott off. He was sobbing, like a stuck record, 'I hate you, I hate you...'

Danny picked himself up, flailing at the air with his fists and hitting his mother instead of Scott. 'I don't want to be your friend any more,' he cried. 'I hate you, too!' Then he turned and ran down the driveway as fast as he could.

From the door Teal ordered, 'Come inside right now, Scott. Julie, you'd better go after Danny—I'll talk to you later.'

She shot a quick glance at the man standing on the porch. His face was set in grim lines, the scrapes and bruises on his cheek making him look like a stranger, someone she'd never known and never would know. Pivoting, she ran after her son.

Danny had headed straight home and was banging in futile rage on the back door. Julie pulled out her keys and said, 'Stop it, Danny—it's okay to be angry but you don't break things. Go indoors and we'll talk when you've calmed down a bit.'

Danny ran for the stairs, scooping up Einstein as he went. Julie locked the back door, sank down on the nearest stool and put her head down on the counter. She had done the stupidest thing in the world: for the second time in her life she had fallen in love with a man who was unreachable. And, once again, her son was paying the price.

CHAPTER NINE

Two hours later the telephone rang. Danny was in bed asleep, worn out by emotion. Einstein, who had allowed himself to be hugged for the better part of an hour, was now outdoors hunting mice. Julie had changed into her housecoat and poured herself a glass of wine in an attempt to relax. That she was now regarding a telephone as if it were a boa constrictor loose in her bedroom proved the futility of her efforts.

Gingerly she picked up the receiver. 'Hello?'

'It's Teal. How's Danny?'

'Asleep. And Scott?'

'The same. Marylee phoned an hour ago—she came into town today and heard about the accident. Scott and I are going back to the cottage with her tomorrow morning to spend a few days there. It'll give me the chance to recuperate and the boys the chance to cool down. So I'll call you when we get back.'

Julie said, quite rationally, 'Do you think that's a good idea?'

'Obviously—or I wouldn't be doing it.'

'You don't think that you're running away from conflict?'

Teal didn't want her opposing the only course of action open to him. 'Our two sons need to learn that they're not the ones calling the shots.'

Also quite rationally, Julie decided to lose her temper. 'So who is calling the shots, Teal? Your parents, who didn't want you? Your wife, who's been dead for two

151

years? Or you, who's scared to death to trust in your emotions?'

'Don't push me, Julie!'

'You're the one who's doing the pushing—pushing me away! You do it all the time.'

Out of some deep place he hadn't even recognized Teal said bluntly, 'When I come back, I think we should end our agreement.'

The words were like a death-knell. Julie's temper died, and into the vacuum rushed terror and despair. Drawing on every scrap of her pride—an emotion a long way from either honesty or courage—she said, 'Fine. Have a good time at the cottage. Goodbye.'

She put the phone back on the hook. After pouring the wine down the bathroom sink, she went to bed and cried herself to sleep.

The next few days were among the worst in Julie's life. Teal's absence made her feel as if one of her limbs had been amputated: she was left with pain and the ghostly memory of what had been.

Adding to her distress, she had to work three straight shifts, which meant leaving Danny with a sitter at a time when he badly needed to be with her; the sensation this gave her was of being torn in two, one part doing her best for her patients, the other frantic to be home with her son. Danny moped around the house, missing Scott, and, so she discovered on the third night, missing more than Scott. She was drying his hair before he went to bed when he said out of the blue, 'Teal's just like my dad.'

Julie's hands stilled. 'What do you mean?'

'He's gone away. Like my dad always did.'

Tears filmed Julie's eyes; she had been crying a lot the last few days. And how could she deny what Danny was saying? It was true. Robert had spent very little time at the old house on the shore. His career had always taken precedence over his family, a career that had progressed steadily from small local theaters to the lights of Broadway. And she now knew that Melissa also had kept him away.

That Danny was suffering as deeply as she galvanized Julie into action. She said, 'Danny, I've got the next four days off. If we can get reservations, would you like to go to Prince Edward Island? We could go to the beach, and see *Anne of Green Gables*, and go to all the amusement parks.'

'When?'

'Tomorrow,' she said recklessly.

'Yeah,' he said, with the first sign of interest he'd shown in anything since Scott had gone away.

As though it was meant to be, everything fell into place. Julie paid for the cottage with the money she had been saving for a down payment on a house, and they caught the ferry to the island the next morning. Danny met other children at the cottages and at the beach, he loved the musical about the little orphan girl with red hair, and three days into their holiday Julie arranged a switch of shifts by long distance so that they could stay an extra day.

Danny looked like a different boy by the time they caught the ferry home. On the outskirts of Halifax they picked up Einstein at the kennels where he had been boarded, and twenty minutes later turned into their driveway.

Einstein had not appreciated his stay at the kennels. He spat at Danny when the boy opened the latch on the cage, and streaked for the bushes in the back garden. Crouched under the lilac, he growled at them, his tail lashing. No doubt he'd dig up some of her flowers in revenge, Julie thought, wishing she could find this funny, and climbed out of the car, stretching her limbs.

She and Danny began carrying their cases and gear into the house, which smelled empty and deserted and gave her very little sense of having come home. None of the messages on her answering machine was from Teal, and her mail was a collection of bills and fliers. Crushed by disappointment, she fought back tears.

What would she do if ending the agreement meant Teal never wanted to see her again? It was the question she had struggled with all the time she was away; the only answer she had reached was that she didn't think she could bear it.

She went back outside to untie the lobster pot they had bought from a fisherman near Souris. She was wrestling with the knots when, with a screech of brakes, a black car pulled up at the end of the driveway. Scott hurtled out of the front seat and ran toward them. He stopped short a couple of feet from Danny, who was trying to do up Einstein's cage again, and said in a rush, 'I'm sorry I was mad at you—I don't hate you. Can we be friends again?'

Danny stood up, his grin exposing a new gap in his teeth. 'Yeah...let's go play in the tree house.'

They ran back down the driveway, Danny yelling on the way, 'Hi, Teal!' Then they were gone and Julie was left with a dark-haired man striding toward her, dressed in an immaculate grey business suit. He must have just come from work, she thought, and wished she didn't look so crumpled and wind-blown.

As he got closer, she saw something else: he was in a towering rage. His face still had not entirely healed, giving him the air of a high-class gangster; she quelled any impulse she might have to giggle. He gripped her by the elbow and said, 'Where the *devil* have you been?'

'I left a message on your machine—we went to PEI.'

'You were supposed to get back yesterday!'

'I changed shifts with one of the other nurses so we could stay another day.'

'Did it occur to you to let me know?'

'No,' she said baldly, 'it didn't. You're the one who doesn't want to get involved—remember?'

'It's too late,' he grated. 'I *am* involved. Whether I want to be or not. The last twenty-four hours have been the longest of my entire life. You'd had a car accident. You'd been abducted. You'd met someone else and married him. For someone who deals in facts, my imagination's had a field day.'

Julie's heart was beating as fast as Einstein's when he was stalking a bird. 'You sure don't look very happy about being involved.'

Biting off the words, he said, 'I was involved once before. It caused me one hell of a lot of grief.'

'Elizabeth . . .'

'Right—Elizabeth. Congratulations, Julie.'

Julie wanted to ask whether he meant grief literally, or whether he had meant misery; the distinction was all-important. She said, 'So what are you going to do about me, Teal?'

'I know what I want to do.'

She remembered those horrible days before she had gone away, and the many hours of her holiday she had spent sunk in despair. 'We both know that,' she stormed. 'You want to end the agreement. Run away and hide so you won't have to change. Well, go ahead. Do it. *I* won't stop you!'

'I want to go to bed with you,' Teal said.

Her jaw dropped. *What*?'

With savage self-contempt he added, 'You'll laugh at me if I say it would take less courage to jump off a hundred-foot cliff.'

Feeling as stunned as if she were the one with the concussion, Julie said, 'No, I won't laugh.'

'Would you go to bed with me, Julie? Would you do that?'

She was still not quite sure she could believe the evidence of her own ears. 'We'd have to end the agreement,' she said foolishly. 'It said no sex.'

'That agreement was one of the stupidest moves I've ever made in my whole life.' He tightened his grasp on her arm. 'For heaven's sake say you'll do it.'

She gave him a small smile. 'I brought you back a present,' she said. 'You can open it when you get home—although make sure Scott's not around. It's my answer to your question.'

Teal scanned her face. He didn't see how a present was much of an answer, and he was desperate to know he hadn't lost her. With a muffled groan he pulled her toward him, lowered his head and began kissing her. For a moment she resisted him. But then to his infinite joy she kissed him back, her body curving to fit his in a way that inflamed him. He muttered against her lips, 'The answer's yes, isn't it? Tell me it's yes...'

She wound her arms around him, felt him flinch with pain and said, horrified, 'I forgot about your ribs—I'm sorry!'

'I forget about them too, until they remind me. You still haven't said yes.'

She reached up and kissed him very explicitly. 'Trust your senses, Teal,' she said.

He hadn't lost her; she still wanted him. Almost dizzy with relief, Teal said, 'Why can't I open your present in front of Scott?'

'Wait and see,' she said with a mischievous grin.

'When are your next days off?' he demanded.

'Not for five days. I owe Shirley a shift.'

'I've waited thirty-four years...why does five days sound like forever?' he said. 'I'd better head home, Julie, and see what the boys are up to.'

'I'm glad they're friends again.'

'Not half as glad as I am.' He kissed her again. 'I don't deserve this—I was a fool to tell you I wanted to end the agreement.'

'It hurt. A lot,' she said honestly.

He had known for weeks that he had the power to arouse her; he had been hiding from the knowledge that he could also hurt her. All the old fears twanged along his nerves. Take her to bed first, Teal, he told himself, and worry about feelings afterwards.

'Have you eaten?' he asked. 'Let me go home and change, and the four of us could go out for dinner.'

'Yes,' said Julie, and smiled at him.

'Every time I'm away from you I forget how beautiful you are,' Teal said roughly, lifting the weight of her hair in his two hands and holding it away from her face. 'I always doubt that you can possibly be as beautiful as I remember.'

Mesmerized by the wonderment in his gray eyes, Julie knew she had been right to risk bringing him home a gift. She smiled at him again, letting her happiness shine in her face.

He said huskily, 'When you look at me like that, everything seems so simple,' and gave her another lingering kiss, nibbling at her lower lip. 'I must go home—how long before you're ready for dinner?'

'Give me an hour.' She stepped back, took a large gift-wrapped box out of the back seat of her car and passed it to him. 'I hope this is what you want,' she said very seriously.

'Why don't I open it right now?'

'Oh, not out here,' she answered in quick alarm.

'Then I'll open it as soon as I get home. See you around seven.' Tucking the box under his arm, he walked back to his car and drove off, waving at her as he went.

Teal wanted to go to bed with her. Maybe as soon as next weekend.

He was involved. Whatever that meant.

Teal drove straight home. The boys were in the tree house. Going up to his bedroom, he undid the ribbon on the box and tore off the flowered paper. Then he opened the lid.

One by one he spread the contents of the box on his bed. A pretty home-made candle. A tape of 'Lara's Theme'. A filmy blue nightgown that made his heart thump in his chest. And finally, attached to a cardboard backing, an advertisement for a cottage by the sea, complete with fireplace and king-sized bed. On the card inside the box Julie had written, 'This gift is for us to share... but only if you want to.'

He was a grown man, he thought numbly. Grown men didn't cry.

Of all the tangled emotions clogging his throat, wonderment and fear were the two uppermost. For Julie's real gift was, of course, herself.

At ten past seven Julie was tapping on Teal's door, wearing a flounced skirt and a ruffled top, her hair loose on her shoulders. Scott opened the door. 'Hi, Julie,' he said and hugged her. 'I missed you.'

She hugged him back. Then Danny came running in, Teal following at a more leisurely pace on his heels. She loved both boys and at the moment would have wished them to be anywhere else but here. The gift which had caused her so much heart-searching now seemed the height of temerity; she was chasing Teal, just like all those other women.

Teal crossed the kitchen floor, kissed her firmly on the mouth and said, 'Ready, guys?'

Julie ushered their two sons out to the car, wondering why falling in love was considered a desirable state of mind. All it was doing to her was tying her stomach in knots.

They ate at a neighborhood steak house and went back to Teal's afterwards. As he poured two brandies, the boys went outside to play flashlight tag in the back garden. Teal raised his glass and said quietly, 'I'd like to share your gift, Julie.'

Her heart gave a panic-stricken lurch. 'Oh,' she said, 'that's nice.'

'If you're free in five days, why don't I make reservations at that new resort that's near Chester? It's only an hour from the city and they have chalets with fireplaces right by the beach.'

'That sounds lovely...but what about the boys?'

While he'd been waiting for her Teal had thought this out. 'Marylee has often offered to take Scott for me. I could ask her if Scott and Danny could stay at the cottage for a couple of days.'

'If she doesn't mind, that would be ideal,' Julie said, and listened to the thrum of her pulse in her ears. This had been her idea in the first place...why was she feeling so afraid?

'Great. I'll call for reservations first thing tomorrow.'

Julie took a big mouthful of brandy and let it burn its way down her throat. She loved Teal. They would have two days together in a secluded cottage with the sound of the sea as their only companion. They would make love, and maybe she would find out what it was that had distanced him so drastically from his sexuality and his emotions. There was no need for her to worry.

She asked some questions about the resort and checked on his calendar to make sure which days she had off. Then the boys came running in, hot, breathless and in dire need of something to drink, and shortly afterwards Julie took Danny home.

As she undressed that night before going to bed, she looked down at herself, her nightgown dangling in one hand. Privately she had always thought her breasts were too full; and there was no question but that her pregnancy had marked her body. Robert had lost interest in her sexually very early in the marriage, although it was only on his last visit to the old house on the shore that she'd discovered he had been having an affair with Melissa for years. If she, Julie, hadn't been woman enough to hold Robert, why should she be able to satisfy a man as complicated as Teal?

She should never have given the gift to him. It was asking for trouble.

Before he left the house the next morning, Teal made reservations for two nights in one of the seaside chalets at the resort. He gave out his VISA number and put down the phone. Not giving himself time to think, he dialed Marylee's number and explained what he wanted.

'We'd be delighted to have the boys,' she said warmly. 'In fact, I was thinking of phoning you. I'm taking Sara and Jane horseback riding after supper this evening, and I thought Scott might like to go, too. Why don't you ask Danny? That way he could meet me and the girls, and he wouldn't be coming to stay with total strangers.'

Inwardly blessing her for her tact and kindness, Teal said, 'That's sweet of you, Marylee...I'll ask Danny. What time?'

'I'd pick them up at six. We wouldn't be home before nine—the stables are out of town; is that too late?'

'I'll call Julie and check with her—I shouldn't think so. Thanks, Marylee...I'll see you at six.'

The die was cast, he thought, putting down the phone. Julie's shift today was seven to seven; he'd phone her from work. He pulled on his jacket, automatically shielding his ribs, and went downstairs to say hello to Mrs Inkpen.

Julie sounded harassed when he spoke to her. 'That's fine,' she said. 'Danny went riding in PEI and loved it. Would you give her whatever money she needs and I'll pay you back...? Okay, Shirley, I'll be right there...I've got to go, Teal, bye.'

Today was Monday. On Saturday he was going to spend two days with the woman he had just spoken to. Two days and two nights, he thought with a dry mouth. Two nights alone with Julie...

His secretary knocked on the door. 'Come in,' Teal said, and with relief submerged himself in the business of the day.

Sharp at six Marylee picked the boys up. Danny was ready and waiting, a plastic bag of carrots tucked under his arm for the horses. Probably Julie's entire supply of carrots, Teal thought drily, waving goodbye and then walking back into his empty house.

Because Mrs Inkpen had done her usual sweep, it was extremely tidy. The flowers Julie had brought had long ago died; as he wandered restlessly from room to room, he decided she was right—the house was colorless. Bleak. Bare. He had never liked minimalist art, so why was he living in a home so denuded of vitality?

So expressive of Elizabeth.

He paused in front of a black and white photograph that had been one of her favorites. An old man was sitting alone on a park bench with a crowd of blank-faced and anonymous people streaming past him. No connections anywhere, Teal thought. Only loneliness and isolation.

But surely Julie was different from everything this photograph expressed. Julie danced as if there were no tomorrow, as if the very essence of joy surged through her veins.

How would she make love? The same way?

On Saturday he'd find out. He'd committed himself to doing so.

Grown men weren't supposed to feel afraid, either.

He collected a bundle of Scott's dirty clothes and started a wash. He made himself a salad and ate it staring out at the garden. He'd feel better if he could mow the lawn or prune the shrubs; but his ribs were still too painful for that. He tried to work, but the tangle of legal words couldn't hold his interest. Finally, at quarter-past eight, he left the house and walked over to Julie's.

He could tell her about their reservations, and that Marylee would keep the boys.

There were lights shining in her windows and through the screen door he could hear Bette Midler singing about the wind beneath her wings. He rang the bell.

Julie came running through the kitchen and unlatched the door, her face alight with pleasure. 'Hi, Teal—come in.'

She was wearing the cut-off denim shorts and halter-top that she had been wearing the first time he had met her. Her legs seemed to go on forever. He said, feeling his blood thicken in his veins, 'I hope you don't mind my dropping in—I wanted to tell you about the reservations.'

Mind? Just the sight of him had made Julie feel as buoyant as one of her birthday balloons. 'It's nice to see you,' she chattered. 'I'm trying to tidy up Danny's room. Three dried-up worms in the pocket of his jeans and I've just found a dead mouse under the bed. Einstein's contribution. You know how I feel about rodents. Yuk.'

It would be all right, Teal thought. She was as different from Elizabeth as she could be. 'Danny's T-shirts always look as though he's slept in the ditch,' he said. 'I'll get rid of the mouse for you if you like.'

'Grab a beer from the fridge and I definitely do like.'

He uncapped the beer and followed her down the hall. Her room was across from Danny's. In a quick glance he saw a bed with a rose-pink spread heaped with lacy cushions, and curtains splashed with exotic tropical flowers. It was a double bed.

Danny's room was decorated in reds and blues; picking his way past the vacuum cleaner and the clothes hamper, he put his beer on the bookshelves and eased himself under the bed. Luckily, for the sake of his ribs, the mouse was within reach. As Julie wrinkled her nose in disgust, he walked past her and went outside to bury it in the garden.

After scrubbing his hands in the kitchen, he went back to the bedroom. Julie had turned off the vacuum cleaner. Picking up the hamper, she headed for the door. But she tripped over the cord, and a motley collection of shorts and socks fell on the floor. 'Darn,' she said, and put the hamper down.

Teal stooped to help her pick up the clothes. They both reached for the same sock, his hand overlying hers. He found himself gripping it, seized by a tension he couldn't have put a name to, and looked up, his eyes meeting the mysterious smoke-blue of hers. And then his gaze dropped, lingering on her cleavage, on the fullness of her breasts under the blue fabric.

'Julie...' he said hoarsely, and leaned forward to kiss her.

Her mouth was soft, welcoming him. Bracing his knee on the carpet, he pulled her closer, teasing her lips open with his tongue. Her skin smelled of soap and her shoulderbones felt fragile under his palms. This is right, he thought dimly. It has to be right.

'Come to bed with me, Julie—now,' he muttered. 'I don't want to wait until the weekend. We've waited long enough.'

'Yes,' she said.

Awkwardly he got to his feet, clasping her hand in his as she led him across the hall. She pulled back the spread, revealing sheets with the same wild pattern of flowers, and then stood still, looking unaccustomedly unsure of herself. Teal unbuttoned his shirt, hearing the tape on his ribcage rasp against it as he pulled it off. Then he eased her top over her head, baring her breasts. His hands not quite steady, he stroked each one to its tip, feeling them tighten at his touch.

And then his control broke. He pulled her down on the bed with him, seeking out her mouth, the curves of her breasts, tangling his legs with the length of hers. Clumsy with haste, he tugged at the zipper on her shorts and shoved the denim down over her hips, intoxicated by the silken warmth of her flesh. It had been too long, he thought, too long since he'd been with a woman, and God, how he wanted her.

As he twisted to get out of his own shorts, his ribs screamed a protest. He ignored them, too intent on plundering all the sweetness of her mouth, his hips already moving against hers as he pressed her down into the mattress. The softness of her breasts crushed to his chest pushed him deeper into the heated, frantic spiral of desire. His heartbeat was pounding in his ears, the blood surging through his body, and his whole world had narrowed to a woman's body on a bed, a woman whose legs had opened to him and whose hips were moving under his in a rhythm too provocative to be denied.

With his fingers he sought out the wetness between her thighs, and in passionate gratitude thrust into her, groaning deep in his throat as she enveloped him. He could feel the pressure mounting unbearably, the throbbing seizing him in its ancient impulsions; before he was ready for it he spilled within her in a tumult of release that took the breath from his body and left him, drained, in that place that was like death.

His eyes were closed and all around him was blackness, desire was gone as if it had been slashed from him with a sword. He was alone, as he had been alone all his life.

Fighting for breath, his head hanging low, he felt words begin to swirl in his brain, words that only served to deepen his isolation; for Julie had been right to guess that he'd lived in a place of loneliness for as long as he could remember. He'd married Elizabeth to get out of it; and instead had found himself mired deeper than before. There was no surcease, he thought in despair. None. The love stories of the world which spoke of unions beyond the physical were just that: stories. Fabrications to console against the darkness of the human spirit.

He pushed himself up on his elbows, feeling the air cool against his skin where Julie's body had warmed him. This is Julie, he thought. Julie lying beneath me. But, the way I treated her, she could have been anyone.

And then, with an irony that he couldn't possibly have explained to her, he realized that he had done nothing to protect her against a pregnancy.

He rolled off her and said in a voice devoid of emotion, 'I shouldn't have done that—I didn't stop to think.'

She was lying very still, the curves of her body gleaming like pearl in the dusky evening light. It took him a moment to see that she was crying, slow, silent tears seeping down her cheeks. She looked bereft. Stunned. Like a woman who had just been told her beloved was dead, he thought—and wondered where such an image had come from.

Elizabeth, once he had climaxed, had wanted nothing more from him. But Julie was weeping. Through the black loneliness Teal felt the first faint stirrings of a feeling different from despair.

In a voice she scarcely recognized as her own, Julie said, 'What shouldn't you have done?'

'I shouldn't have made love to you.'

'You didn't.'

Her honesty flicked him on the raw. Anger was an emotion he knew; gratefully he embraced it. 'That's right—I didn't. You could have been anyone—which is the reason I've been fighting you off all summer.'

She sat up on the bed, ignoring the tears hanging on her lashes, her nostrils flared. 'Oh, so now it's my fault?'

He hauled himself upright. 'No, damn it, it's my fault! Why the devil do you think I wanted the agreement in the first place? To keep me out of situations like this, of course.'

'You don't have to swear,' she snapped.

He raked his hair back from his forehead. 'You have my full permission to cancel out of this weekend.'

She said levelly, 'I wanted to make love with you more than anything else in the world. But all I feel now is used. Used and tossed aside.'

'That's all I'm capable of giving!'

'Then you're just like Robert,' Julie said.

He felt as if she'd hit him in the ribs with the bedpost. 'You hated sex with Robert.'

'That's right.' Her fists clenched impotently, she said, 'What's the good of my being beautiful and sexy-looking? So what if every date I have wants to take me to bed? It doesn't do me any good—no one ever sees me as a real person. Sex is using people—just like you used me.'

Utterly appalled, Teal whispered, 'Julie, I'm sorry...'

He wasn't sure she'd even heard him. She went on in the same dead voice, 'If you can't give more of yourself than you just did, I'm not going anywhere with you this weekend.'

The stab of pain in Teal's chest had nothing to do with his ribs. He said clumsily, 'I hurt you—I didn't mean to do that.'

If anything, she looked even more stricken. 'This is the end, isn't it? We're through with each other.'

She was sitting only inches from him, naked, her hair tumbled on her shoulders, her cheeks drained of color. For the second time in minutes Teal's breathing stopped in his throat; into the silence the antique clock in the living-room began to chime.

Julie's eyes widened in shock. 'It's nine o'clock,' she gasped, scrambling off the bed and reaching for her clothes. 'Marylee will be bringing the boys back any minute.'

He took her by the arm. 'We can't leave this——'

'Teal, the boys will be home soon,' she repeated furiously. 'They sure don't need to find us in bed together;

they're confused enough as it is. Let go of me! And for heaven's sake put something on!'

His clothes seemed to be scattered all over the floor; he had no recollection of how they'd got there. As Julie fled from the room, he began to get dressed, struggling to sort out his feelings even as his fingers wrestled with the buttons on his shirt.

Out of his confusion one thought surfaced. He couldn't walk out of this house and never hold Julie in his arms again. He couldn't bear that.

He followed her down the hall to the bathroom, where she was splashing cold water on her face, and said hoarsely, 'We've got to talk——'

'I don't think so,' she said tightly. 'Sometimes actions speak louder than words.'

'I'm not leaving you like this!'

'You don't have any choice. I'm going outside to wait for Danny, and I'm certainly not going to be in the middle of a fight with you when he arrives.'

What was wrong with him? He felt tongue-tied, his brain reduced to mush. Mr Chief Justice Mersey wouldn't recognize him, Teal thought fleetingly, and in the mirror saw a stranger looking back at him, a man he scarcely recognized.

Julie had already gone down the hall. Trying to get a grip on himself, Teal went outside. She was sitting on the only chair on the porch, Einstein clutched to her breast; two pairs of eyes, one smoke-blue, the other amber, regarded him with equal animosity. Her fingers were clenched in Einstein's fur, and he could see the hammer-beat of her pulse at the base of her throat.

She was certainly angry with him, Teal was in no doubt about that. But beneath a surface bravado he sensed that she was also frightened. Terrified out of her wits. Praying that he was right, he announced with all the violence of suppressed emotion and no diplomacy whatsoever, 'I'll pick you up on Saturday after lunch.'

'I'm not going.'

'Yes, you are! You were crying, Julie—what I do matters to you; I'm finally starting to figure that out. All I'm asking for is a second chance—I promise there'll be no repeat of what happened tonight.'

Rubbing Einstein's skull with fierce concentration, Julie said raggedly, 'What if you really are like Robert? I couldn't bear to go through that again.'

Teal put all the force of his personality into his words. 'I'm not—I swear I'm not.'

'I don't know anything any more,' she said hopelessly, her shoulders drooping.

Behind him a car turned into the driveway. Teal said urgently, 'You're going with me on the weekend, Julie.'

Not looking at him, she muttered, 'All right—I'll go.'

Light-headed with relief, Teal turned around as the four children erupted from the car, and somehow managed to conduct a coherent conversation with Marylee in the kitchen. There was no further opportunity to speak to Julie alone, nor did he try to engineer one. Half an hour later he and Scott walked home together.

He had Julie's promise that she'd go away with him on Saturday.

The rest was up to him.

CHAPTER TEN

TEAL and Julie arrived at the resort late in the afternoon. Julie had worked an overnight shift and had gone to bed at seven-thirty that morning to get some sleep. At least, that had been the theory, she thought as Teal parked in front of a log-faced chalet and she climbed out of the car. She had been too on edge to sleep well, and now was a mass of nerves.

The chalet was surrounded by fragrant balsam fir and silver-trunked birches, through which she glimpsed the vibrant blue of the sea. The waves sloshed against the rocks with a repetitive, soothing rhythm, while the boughs of the trees swayed back and forth in the breeze. She and Teal were enclosed in a small private world, and as she filled her lungs with the salt air she felt a slight lessening of the tension that had been with her ever since she'd allowed Teal into her bed last Monday night.

Why had she done that? And why had she let him talk her into coming here?

'What a beautiful place,' she said banally.

Teal was getting their cases out of the back seat. He could only lift with one hand; she grabbed her own bag, waited as he unlocked the door of the chalet and followed him inside.

At any other time the room would have delighted her. A bouquet of garden flowers stood on the coffee-table in front of the stone fireplace, the picture window overlooked the ocean, and the bed—a very large bed—had an attractive forest-green spread that blended with the lighter green carpet.

Teal put his case down and went back outside, returning a moment later with the gift box she had given him. Without saying a word he placed the candle beside the bed, put her nightgown on the pillow and inserted the tape of 'Lara's Theme' into his portable tape deck. The plaintive melody filled the room. He said quietly, 'Come to bed with me, Julie.'

Instinctively he had done exactly the right thing. How could she go for a walk with him along the shore, or play tennis, or have a drink at the bar in the main lodge when part of her craved to be held by him and the rest of her wanted to run a mile from the big bed?

She smiled with stiff lips and picked up the blue nightgown. 'I won't be a minute.'

The bathroom was luxuriously appointed. Julie undressed, slid the gown over her head, brushed her hair loose and sprayed on some of her most expensive perfume to give herself courage. Courage. She was beginning to hate that word.

She met her eyes in the mirror. I love Teal, she thought. I love him. Everything will be all right.

When she went back into the room he had drawn the curtains and stripped to his briefs. The candle was burning with a pure, still flame by the bed. She had no idea what he was thinking, still less what he might be feeling. She was walking into the unknown, toward a man who in so many ways was still a mystery to her, and held tightly to the surety of her love.

Teal watched her come toward him. Even in the small light that the candle cast he could see the outline of her body beneath the filmy blue gown. She was walking tall, all her courage in her eyes; she deserved another orchid, he thought. A whole bouquet of orchids.

Since Monday he had rehearsed any number of fancy speeches and romantic gestures that he'd hoped would please her. As she stopped in her tracks four feet away from him, he forgot them all and said harshly, 'I don't understand why you're here, Julie—not after the way I've treated you.'

She gave him a blank look. 'Because I love you, of course. Hadn't you figured that out?'

Teal felt as though she'd punched him in the gut; at his involuntary indrawn breath his ribs knifed a protest. 'No,' he said in magnificent understatement, 'I hadn't figured that out.'

'Well, now you know.'

She wasn't nearly as at ease as she was trying to sound; a muscle was twitching in her jaw and her eyes were looking anywhere in the room but at him. These tiny betrayals filled Teal with the same emotions he'd felt when he'd first held Scott in his arms: both an over-whelming tenderness at the mystery and wonder of another human being, and a sense of the utter incommunicability of that tenderness.

He closed the distance between them, resting his hands lightly on Julie's shoulders. 'I've done nothing to warrant that.'

'Love isn't earned,' she said helplessly. 'It just is.'

'And what about lovemaking?'

Feeling absurdly shy, Julie slid her hands up Teal's chest, playing with the edge of the tape on his ribs as she sought for words. 'I'm no expert,' she said. 'Far from it. I—I guess what I want is togetherness. No barriers. No separations. The two of us as close as we can possibly be.' Very carefully she pressed down on the corner of the tape, where it had come unstuck. 'I might as well tell you I have no idea how to go about that.'

Neither did he. But, as her perfume drifted to his nostrils, one thing was crystal-clear to him. Julie was open to him. As open as Elizabeth had been closed. Although he could easily have given these words a sexual connotation, he didn't mean them that way. He was important to her, he thought painfully. What he did could affect her, for better or for worse.

This wasn't just about his hang-ups. Julie had her own demons as well. She was a woman whose beauty touched him to the heart; yet this beauty had never brought her the sexual pleasure to which she was entitled.

If he was here to be healed, so also was she.

He said at random, 'Last time I did nothing to protect you from pregnancy.'

'I'm on the Pill because I've been having trouble with my periods,' she said, and crinkled her nose at him. 'Just as well, wouldn't you say? I don't think, right now, that we need the complication of a baby.'

His voice sounding strange in his ears, Teal said, 'We're here for us, then. Just us.'

'No "just" about it,' she said vigorously. 'Of course we're here for us—who else would we be here for?'

Forcing himself to lower the first of the barriers, knowing he was stepping from long-familiar territory into the unknown, Teal took a deep breath and said, 'The only reason Elizabeth wanted to go to bed with me—ever—was to get pregnant.'

The shock of his disclosure ran through Julie's body. For a moment she scarcely believed it, so alien was it to the way she felt about Teal. But then, meeting his eyes, she saw that it was indeed true. She said strongly, 'I'm not Elizabeth. I want you—right here and now—for yourself.'

Blushing, but refusing to let her eyes drop, she rested her hands on his shoulders, molding the strongly carved muscles. 'Your body is beautiful to me, Teal.' A tiny smile tilted her mouth. 'You wouldn't believe some of the dreams I've had about you.'

It never occurred to him to disbelieve her. Like a man learning a new skill, his first movements tentative and uncertain, he reached out one hand and traced the planes of her cheekbone and the gentle inward line of her cheek. 'I never could reach Elizabeth,' he confessed. 'Not once in seven years of marriage, not even when Scott was born, did she share herself with me. Her core, her essence—she kept those to herself and wouldn't let me in.'

'The place of loneliness,' Julie said softly.

He nodded, grateful for her understanding. 'You're very different from her. I need you, Julie.'

He had never thought to say those words to a woman—and found he had spoken them almost naturally, for their time had come. Julie felt tears film her eyes. In a choked voice she said, 'As we're into confessions, Robert never needed me—or Danny—any more than Elizabeth needed you. Our whole marriage was an act, a sham from beginning to end. For him it was like a dress rehearsal where he could practise extending his emotional range—he used to pick fights with me and then stand back and watch my reactions as though I were a bug on a pin. I hated it!'

Teal didn't even have to think about his next words. 'You're absolutely real to me, Julie. Yes, I find you beautiful—heart-stoppingly beautiful; I'd be a liar if I pretended otherwise—but it's your courage and passion and honesty that——' His voice faltered, then gained strength. 'That I'm in love with.'

She blinked. 'What did you say?'

'I'm in love with you,' Teal said. Throwing back his head, he gave an exultant laugh. 'What a fool I've been! It's been staring me in the face ever since I met you. Julie, darling, dearest Julie, I love you.'

His movements not at all uncertain of themselves, Teal took her face in his hands and kissed her. She looked dazed, her body tense with shock, so that she felt like a mannequin in his arms; he set out to show her that he'd meant every word he'd said. Gentling his kiss, he let his lips play with hers, brushing against them as delicately as the touch of a butterfly, his tongue teasing their softness until he felt their first, almost shy response.

Her palms glided down his chest. 'Am I dreaming?' she whispered. 'Did you say you loved me?'

Laughter warming his voice, Teal said, 'Sweetheart, despite having worked the night shift, you're wide awake. And yes, I do love you.'

'I love you, too!' Julie exclaimed. In all her fantasizing about the weekend, she had not once dreamed of hearing Teal say those words. She looped her arms around his neck, her eyes dancing. 'You know what? I'm not nearly as scared as I was five minutes ago.'

Teal had never thought laughter could be a part of lovemaking. 'You're not begging for mercy? Julie, you disappoint me.'

She let one hand wander further down his body. 'It's not mercy I'm begging for, Teal Carruthers.'

'Are you telling me I talk too much?' he growled, steering her toward the bed, pulling back the covers and lying down beside her on the cool sheets. He said, no longer laughing, 'We have two days together. Two whole days. We have all the time in the world to learn how to please each other.'

'There's nothing I would rather do,' Julie said.

The intensity that was so much a part of her shone from her eyes, and in them, mysteriously, he caught a gleam of the same blue that was at the base of the candle-flame. Although his heart was racing and he desired her as fiercely as a caged man craved freedom, he deliberately restrained himself. Because Julie wanted something from him. Something far more complex than the child Elizabeth had wanted. Julie wanted all of him, body and soul, his emotions, his laughter and his tears. She wanted intimacy—the one thing Elizabeth had shunned.

He began stroking the length of her body under the filmy nightgown, learning the flow from breast to waist to hip to thigh, the geography of flesh and bone that was Julie. He took the weight of her breasts in his hands, teasing their tips to hardness, intoxicated by the sensual slide of the pale blue fabric over her skin, now hiding, now revealing. He buried his face in the shining fall of her hair, ran his mouth down her throat to the rise of her breast, tasting her, and then let his fingers drift between her thighs, tangled in the slippery folds of her gown.

Her indrawn breath echoed his own. He looked up. Although she had been lying still, it was as far from the stillness of passivity as it could be. Her eyes, brilliant with desire, were trained on his, and the soft, voluptuous curve of her mouth spoke volumes; for a moment that was out of time her image filled his vision and he knew he would never forget this instant when, unfulfilled, he was certain he could both find and give fulfillment.

She leaned forward, pulling the nightgown over her head in a graceful flash of bare arms, her nakedness touching him to the core. Then she reached over and pulled his briefs down over his hips. 'Lie still, Teal,' she whispered. 'It's my turn.'

He lay back on the sheets, aware with some distant part of his brain that she wanted him to expose his vulnerability as much as his body. Lying down beside him, her breasts moving gently in the candlelight, she touched him with hands and mouth and body until he thought he would die with the pleasure of it. And finally, as he had been longing for her to do, she slid her thighs between his and with the fingers of one hand encircled the hardness that was all his pent-up need of her.

He groaned her name as the dark throbbing spread to encompass his whole body. 'Not yet, Julie—not yet,' he muttered, and rolled over, remembering at the last moment to protect his ribs. Parting her thighs, he began playing with her with an exquisite gentleness; she was as sleek and wet as a sea creature, her body arching with pleasure like a dolphin's in the waves of the ocean. As she pulled him closer, forgetting to be gentle, he felt a flood of primitive power that he could so move her. She was his. His mate. His woman. His love.

In her eyes and in the long line of her throat he sensed the storm gathering within her, and knew that his one desire was to release that storm. Bringing all his imagination and his new-found love to the task, he watched her throw her head back, her belly a taut curve.

Then suddenly she broke, crying out his name over and over again in a litany that filled Teal with a strange mixture of pride and humility. As she collapsed in his arms, her breathing as rapid as a child's, he felt again that upwelling of tenderness. But this time he could communicate it: he had the words. The simplest, most profound words in the language.

'Julie, I love you,' he said.

Her lashes fluttered open. She took his palm and laid it against her breast so that he could feel the triphammer of her heartbeat, and whispered, 'Dearest Teal...I love you, too.'

For a few moments she was still, lost in the place to which he had taken her. He let his mouth drift over her drowned face and the sweet curves of her body, content to wait for her because there was all the time in the world and she was his, his beautiful Julie.

His head was resting on her breast. Toying with the silky thickness of his hair, Julie murmured, 'I feel very happy.' She let her hands wander the length of his spine, almost idly at first. Then they moved lower, to his hips and buttocks. Suddenly her body twisted, and with a blatant eroticism that seared Teal like fire she pulled him on top of her, opening her legs to gather him in. 'Now,' she said fiercely. 'Now, Teal.'

He thrust deep into her body, rearing up on his elbows to drink in all the fleeting expressions on her face. 'I don't want this to be over,' he said roughly.

She arched her hips under him and his face convulsed. 'Teal,' she said, 'this is just the beginning...I'm not going to go away. Not if you don't want me to.'

Open to him. Wanting him. 'I don't want you to go away. Ever,' he said, and lowered his weight on her, kissing her with a passion that had lain dormant within him for years. It had taken Julie to release it, he thought. The gift she had really given him was himself. His true self. The man he had always had the potential to be.

Fueled by gratitude and love, guided by a new-born intuition of what pleased her, he roamed her body; and all the while he moved inside her, wanting fervently to give her pleasure.

In a broken voice he hadn't heard before, she said, 'Please, Teal...oh, please.' Only then did he let go, allowing the urgent demands of his body to overwhelm him and trusting that somehow that was what she wanted too.

She cried out, sharp and fierce as a seabird; he emptied within her even as the tension in her body throbbed its way to satiation. One flesh, Teal thought. So that's what that means. I never knew.

His chest was heaving, and the beating of his heart could have been her own. He smoothed her hair back from her face and said, struggling for breath, 'What I feel now is the very opposite of loneliness.'

She wound her arms around him. 'When we're truly together, how can we be lonely?'

The candle was still burning by the bedside. His voice husky with emotion, Teal said, 'You've given me the most wonderful gift in the world.'

She smiled at him, snuggling a little closer, and rested her cheek on his shoulder. Within minutes she was asleep. But Teal stayed awake, listening to the peaceful rhythm of her breathing, letting the joy and trust that she had brought him settle quietly in his heart.

They made love again when Julie awoke, ordered Room Service for dinner because neither of them wanted any company other than their own, played in the Jacuzzi after they had eaten, and somehow found themselves locked in an embrace against the bathroom door. Julie started to giggle. 'You're a sex maniac,' she said.

'Are you complaining?'

With an abrupt change of mood she said seriously, 'I've loved every minute we've spent here.' Her brow wrinkled. 'I've seen a side of you I only caught glimpses of before—I wasn't always sure it existed because you were so controlled. So determined to keep me at a distance.'

In less than eight hours in a chalet by the sea Teal knew his whole life had shifted. He took a fleecy towel from the pile on the shelf and started drying Julie's body, already so well-known to him, so endlessly a source of delight.

He said soberly, 'Elizabeth's dead, and I sometimes think her loneliness must have been as great if not greater than mine... although I'll never know that now.

'I loved her when we married. I knew she wanted children, and that was fine with me. I soon found out that she didn't like sex, but I was young and I figured that would change with time. Scott was born, and from the first moment I saw him I loved him and understood that with him, at least, I didn't have to feel alone. Because you were right—my parents didn't want me; I was just a pawn in their ongoing battle.'

He smoothed the towel down her hips. 'Elizabeth wanted another child. Right away. I went along with that; I thought a daughter would be lovely. But it didn't happen. A year went by, then two. Elizabeth started going to doctors and, because I knew how important it was to her, I went too. There was nothing wrong with me, I was told. Somehow—and this was her word—the fault was hers.'

His hands grew still. The bathroom door was made of pine; he focussed on the knots and whorls in the wood and went on with his story.

'She was desperate, so we tried everything, going from clinic to clinic and doctor to doctor. Elizabeth had never liked being touched; in bed she never let herself go—she was afraid to, I think. All her energy was focussed on getting pregnant—so sex became totally mechanical, tied to temperature and position and timing. No spontaneity, and certainly no love. I got so I loathed it.'

He grimaced. 'Sometimes I wanted to leave her. But how could I when her need was so enormous and when we had Scott to bind us together? And then, of course, she died.'

He pushed himself back, bending his neck to relieve the tightness of his muscles.

'I grieved for her. Of course I did; we'd lived together for seven years and she was the mother of my son, and if I'd fallen out of love with her she was still my wife and far too young to die. But mingled with the grief was tremendous guilt that I'd failed her by never being able to reach her—somehow I should have been able to do so.

'I think the worst thing of all, though, buried underneath everything else, was a feeling of relief.' He suddenly banged his fist against the door-frame, glad of the pain. 'Sheer, simple relief. How could I admit that to anyone? I've never told another living soul, not even Bruce and Marylee.'

But he had told her. Instantly certain that it had been the guilt and the relief, rather than the grief, that had kept him so distanced, so far away from her, Julie said, 'You must have tried to reach Elizabeth.'

'Yeah, I tried. And I failed.'

'She has to bear some of the responsibility for that.'

'Lovemaking didn't reach her and Scott's birth made no difference, so I tried anger—but she wouldn't fight with me,' he said, running his fingernail down the pine panels. 'She just retreated into silence. A silence that could go on for days. God, how I hated that.'

'No wonder you shied like a half-broken horse every time a woman talked commitment.' Julie reached up and lightly touched his mouth. 'The agreement makes a lot more sense now.'

'Logically it made sense.' He smiled crookedly. 'From the moment I first saw you I think my subconscious knew I needed you...and the agreement was how it went about getting you.'

Julie said forthrightly, 'You've broken the pattern of your marriage with me. We've never been either silent or superficial with each other—no matter how hard we tried.'

'It was your honesty that first attracted me.' For the first time since he had started talking to her, Teal smiled. 'Well, that and your cleavage.'

She laughed, letting the towel slide to the floor. 'Let's go to bed.'

'Again?' Teal said. 'I'm not the only sex maniac around here.'

'Beds can be for sleeping, too.'

He said, because he knew it was important, 'I'm glad I told you about Elizabeth...I wanted you to understand. And I want you to feel free to talk about Robert— he's Danny's father, he exists. And I do want us to break the patterns, Julie. You're far too important to me for it to be otherwise.'

She gave him an impish smile. 'I don't hate sex any more.'

'I rather noticed that.' He let his eyes travel the length of her body with a leisurely sensuality. 'What was that you said about sleeping? I'm not sure sleep is my main priority right now.'

'I'm used to night shifts,' Julie said, tangling her fingers in his body hair. 'Let's light a fire in the fireplace.'

'And then we'll light another one in the bed,' Teal said.

Which they did.

Teal pulled up by his house at seven on Monday evening, an hour later than had been planned. Marylee's car was already in the driveway. 'Back to normality,' he said as the boys raced down the steps to meet them.

'I feel as though we've been away for weeks,' Julie responded, and opened her door for Danny's hug. 'Hello, sweetie, how are you?'

Marylee came wandering down the steps. 'Did you have a good time?' she said innocently.

Julie blushed. Teal said with considerable panache, 'Superb. How was the cottage?'

'Wonderful. They want to go back next weekend—if you're interested.'

Julie blushed even redder; amused, Teal came to her rescue. 'I'm sure that could be arranged,' he remarked. 'Want to carry my bag in, Scott?'

'What was the resort like, Julie?' Marylee asked. 'I've heard the beach is beautiful.'

Julie hadn't gone near the beach. 'The dining-room was very attractive,' she said weakly.

'The rocks were gray, the sea was blue and the beach was made of sand,' Teal said. 'Come on in for a drink, Marylee.'

They drank vodka and orange under the maple tree, after which Marylee left. The boys had a tendency to hover; apart from the hours she spent at work Julie was almost never away from Danny. 'I think you missed us,' she said.

The boys exchanged a conspiratorial glance. 'Sort of,' Danny said. 'We got a surprise for you.'

'Yeah,' Scott said. 'In the basement.'

Teal raised his brow. 'Is the lawnmower broken again?'

'Nope.' Scott looked over at Danny, who was stifling a giggle. 'Hurry up and finish your drink, Dad, so we can show you.'

Teal tossed back the last of his vodka. 'Let's go.'

They all went inside. At the top of the basement stairs the boys stood back and Danny said, 'The surprise is in the corner by the furnace—you'll really like it. But you both got to go and see it. Together.'

'Does it bite?' Julie said suspiciously.

This time Scott was the one to collapse into giggles. 'It's okay, Mum,' Danny said kindly. 'Anyway, Teal'll protect you.'

'You haven't come up with a stray dog, Danny? You know Mrs LeMarchant won't let us keep a dog.'

'Go see,' Scott said with another fit of laughter.

Julie gave Teal a mystified look. Teal shrugged his shoulders; he had no more idea than she what this was about. 'After you,' he said.

She went down the stairs cautiously. The basement was full of shadows and very untidy: Mrs Inkpen clearly didn't make it this far. Crossing the floor, she headed for the far corner, Teal close on her heels. Then she heard the door at the top of the stairs slam shut and the metallic screech of the bolt. Teal said, perplexed, 'What are those two up to?'

Julie didn't like basements. Fire in her eye, she marched back up the stairs and said, 'Danny, let us out of here.' The only response was more laughter. She rattled the handle, but the door held firm.

'Did you look by the furnace?' Danny asked.

From the bottom of the stairs Teal called, 'Come and look at this, Julie. I think we've been handed an ultimatum.'

She tramped down the steps. 'Does your basement have rats?' she asked militantly.

'I've never seen one,' Teal answered, grinning at her. 'Once Einstein moves in, we certainly won't have any.'

She frowned at him, her hands on her hips. 'I know you didn't get too much sun the last two days because we never went out in it,' she said. 'What are you talking about? Danny wouldn't part with Einstein.'

'Darling Julie, I think I must have told you I loved you at least once an hour on the hour the whole time we were away. But do you know what I didn't do?'

'Take me for a walk on the beach,' she said promptly.

'I didn't ask you to marry me.'

In the light filtering through the small windows set high in the cement walls Julie could see that he was smiling; but his eyes were intent on her face, and the expression in them made her knees weak. 'You scarcely had time,' she said. 'I kept hauling you off to bed.'

'Will you marry me, Julie?'

She smiled back. 'You must love me if you're willing to take on Einstein.'

'Answer the question, Mrs Ferris,' he ordered in his best courtroom manner.

'Yes, Teal, I'll marry you. I'd really like to. Although we'll have to draw up a new agreement—one that includes sex.'

'I'll make it a priority.' He took her in his arms and kissed her at some length. 'What an innovative and enjoyable way to seal a contract,' he murmured. 'I can't have you disliking lawyers if you're going to marry one.'

Feeling joy bubble up within her, Julie said, 'So what was the boys' surprise?'

From his trouser pocket Teal took out a much creased piece of paper. 'We want you to get maried,' Scott had printed in big red letters. 'We'll let you out wen you agre.'

Underneath, Danny's neater script said, 'Bread and water by the furnace. There's no rats, Mum. We checked.'

She said severely, 'I'm greatly disillusioned. You're only asking me to marry you to avoid a diet of bread and water.'

'Actually I'm hoping that if they live together your son's ability to spell will rub off on mine,' Teal replied.

Then, as she had freed him to do, he gave all his emotions free rein. 'I love you, I need you, I want you,' he said. 'Which has nothing to do with our two sons or with bread and water. As well you know. We could get a special license and get married by the end of the month.'

'Okay,' said Julie.

'Good,' said Teal, and kissed her again. 'Now shall we let the boys know? Or should we let them suffer for a while?'

She glanced around her. 'Even though from now on I'll feel differently about basements, having been proposed to in one, I'm not averse to vacating it as soon as possible.'

He took her by the hand and led her up the stairs. 'We're going to get married,' he said loudly. 'You can let us out now.'

'That didn't take long,' Danny said through the door. 'We were going to starve you into submission, like that movie we saw with all the old knights and barons.'

'That's neat!' Scott crowed. 'Where's the key, Danny?'

'You've got it.'

'No, I don't, I gave it to you.'

'It's not in my pocket.'

'Maybe it's on the picnic table.'

'We'd better go look.'

In the cramped space at the top of the stairs Teal took Julie into his arms. 'We might as well enjoy ourselves while we're waiting,' he said.

Four weeks later Einstein took possession of Teal's garden. He liked it better than the one he had just left; it definitely had more possibilities.

Coming Next Month

HARLEQUIN PRESENTS®

#1767 PRINCE OF DARKNESS Kate Proctor
Damian Sheridan held the key to Ros's past.... But if he discovered her dark secret, would he believe Ros was just an innocent pawn in a game of deceit?

#1768 STRAW ON THE WIND Elizabeth Power
Rex Templeton was rich, gorgeous, charismatic. But he was also paralyzed from the waist down. Could Sasha convince him he was worthy of love?

#1769 THE ALEXAKIS BRIDE Anne McAllister
(Wedlocked!)
Damon Alexakis needed a suitable wife—and Kate needed a pretend lover to keep her matchmaking father happy! The solution? A marriage of convenience for one year only!

#1770 A MASTERFUL MAN Lindsay Armstrong
Davina's handsome new boss, Steve Warwick, was clearly interested in more than Davina's housekeeping skills; could she resist his masterful persuasion?

#1771 CLIMAX OF PASSION Emma Darcy
(Dangerous Liaisons)
When the Sheikh of Xabia accused Amanda of using him to clear her father's name, Amanda proposed a dangerous bargain: one night of love in return for her freedom!

#1772 FANTASIES & AND THE FUTURE Miranda Lee
(Book 4 of Hearts of Fire)
The fourth in a compelling six-part saga—discover the passion, scandal, sin and hope that exist between two fabulously rich families.

Vince Morelli thought Ava was just another rich, lonely housewife looking for fun and thrills! But Ava knew her narrow, virginal existence was gone forever.... Vince was more exciting than any of her fantasies! Life was changing for Gemma, too, but seemingly for the worse: she'd heard evil rumors about Nathan—could they be true?

Take 4 bestselling love stories FREE

Plus get a FREE surprise gift!

Become a Privileged Woman,
You'll be entitled to all these Free Benefits. And Free Gifts, too.

To thank you for buying our books, we've designed an exclusive FREE program called *PAGES & PRIVILEGES™*. You can enroll with just one Proof of Purchase, and get the kind of luxuries that, until now, you could only read about.

BIG HOTEL DISCOUNTS

A privileged woman stays in the finest hotels. And so can you—at up to 60% off! Imagine standing in a hotel check-in line and watching as the guest in front of you pays $150 for the same room that's only costing you $60. Your *Pages & Privileges* discounts are good at Sheraton, Marriott, Best Western, Hyatt and thousands of other fine hotels all over the U.S., Canada and Europe.

FREE DISCOUNT TRAVEL SERVICE

A privileged woman is always jetting to romantic places.

When <u>you</u> fly, just make one phone call for the lowest published airfare at time of booking— <u>or double the difference back!</u>

PLUS—you'll get a $25 voucher to use the first time you book a flight AND <u>5% cash back on every ticket you buy thereafter through the travel service!</u>